THE
EAGLE

WHO IS THE TRAITOR AMONG US?

TRAIL

ROBERT RIGBY

**WALKER
BOOKS**

First published 2014 by Walker Books Ltd
87 Vauxhall Walk, London SE11 5HJ

This edition published 2014

2 4 6 8 10 9 7 5 3 1

Text © 2014 Robert Rigby
Young man photograph © Getty Images, Inc
German infantrymen photograph © PA Photos Limited
Golden Eagle photograph © iStockphoto LP.

The right of Robert Rigby to be identified as author of this work has been
asserted by him in accordance with the Copyright, Designs and Patents Act 1988.

This book has been typeset in M Times New Roman

Printed and bound in Great Britain by Clays Ltd, St Ives plc

British Library Cataloguing in Publication Data:
a catalogue record for this book is available from the British Library

ISBN 978-1-4063-4666-4

www.walker.co.uk

To G

PROLOGUE

Southern France, late August, 1940

The leader of the Andorrans was built like a bull, but he moved with the lightness of a mountain goat. Not once had he stumbled or tripped as he led the small group further and deeper into the towering Pyrenees.

They were high now, long clear of the winding footpaths through the birch forests, way past the rows of mighty beech and the plunging, thundering waterfalls. Here it was quiet, eerily quiet. Here there were few trees, the air was thinner and the paths narrow and steep. Here the ascent was over jagged fragments of rock and long scars of loose scree, which shifted dangerously underfoot, digging into the soles of heavy boots or flimsy, unsuitable shoes. Shoes like the three pampered Parisians wore.

But the Andorran and his two countrymen didn't care about the Parisians or the state of their feet. All they cared about was the money they were being paid to take them – the little Jewish man, his wife and their twelve-year-old son – over the mountains and into Spain, and freedom. Escaping

7

France while they still could. Escaping the Nazis and their distant camps of death.

This was not the first time the Andorrans had trodden this route with frightened escapees, and it would not be the last. Business was brisk. War was not bad for everyone. There were rich pickings for the enterprising.

The early evening was warm, though soon the warmth would go as the sun dipped behind the peaks. They had been lucky with the weather; no driving rain to soak them through, or low, swirling cloud to swallow the pathways. Instead, on both days, the sun had blazed kindly in clear, cloudless skies.

At the head of the line, the bull-like Andorran stopped and turned. He lifted the leather strap running from shoulder to waist to free the shotgun he wore slung across his back.

"Stop here," he said to the family. "Rest. Eat."

The Parisians nodded, father and son sinking gratefully to the ground while the woman delved into her bag to bring out their meagre provisions.

The Andorrans moved away a little, rested their shotguns against a massive slab of fallen limestone and began rolling cigarettes, muttering to each other in low voices. Soon, the acrid smell of their black tobacco drifted on the air.

They watched the Parisians eating, the man chewing slowly, the woman giving most of her share to the boy, who greedily devoured whatever came his way; cheese, a slice of meat, crusts of stale bread, his tongue flicking out to snatch the last crumbs from his chubby fingers.

Taking another deep drag at his cigarette, the Andorran leader licked his dry lips and blew a long stream of smoke from deep in his lungs. He coughed loudly, rolled a thick globule of phlegm around his mouth and spat it onto the ground. The woman stared but quickly looked away as he caught her eye. For her, at least, the Andorran felt some grudging admiration. She had not complained once, unlike the whining twelve year old and the wheedling husband.

The boy had grizzled constantly that he was tired and needed to rest – apart from when he was eating. And the nervous husband, with his suit and raincoat, hat, gold-rimmed glasses and brown leather case – he was a moaner too.

None of it mattered to the Andorrans. They simply ignored it. They knew the leather case contained the family's remaining wealth. Jewellery, no doubt; perhaps even gold. And cash – their cash had to be in the case too. That was why it never left the man's side.

With another loud cough, the Andorran took a final drag on his cigarette and threw down the butt, grinding it into the earth with the sole of his boot.

Suddenly a terrifying, piercing scream rang out and echoed across the narrow valley, seeming to bounce off the rock faces surrounding them.

The Jewish man froze and the boy grasped his mother's arm and cried out, "Mamma!"

But the woman remained calm, quickly seeing that the

Andorrans had not flinched at the sound of the scream. There could be nothing to fear, for them at least.

A shape passed in front of the sun and they glimpsed a moving shadow cast on the craggy rocks opposite. The scream came again, even more agonized this time.

And then they saw it. High above the rising shadow, an eagle flew towards a peak. In the bird's talons, a marmot writhed and shrieked. As they watched, the screaming stopped, the animal went limp, and the eagle continued majestically upwards.

Muttering something to his friends, the leader of the Andorrans beckoned to the Parisian, who was clutching his leather case like a shield against his rigid body.

Much of their communication had been though signs and gestures, as the Andorrans' mix of Catalan, Spanish and rural southern French was as puzzling to the Parisian family as their standard French was to their guides.

Before they left Saint-Girons, the Parisian had tried to tell the Andorrans about the long and anxious flight south; about being smuggled across the Demarcation Line into the Free Zone, and the nerve-jangling train journeys to Toulouse, Carcassonne, Foix, and finally Saint-Girons, where they waited to be met. And, all the while, the accompanying fear, the dread that at any moment their forged papers and passports would be too closely scrutinized.

"This has already cost a small fortune," he had moaned, handing over to the Andorran leader the thick wad of banknotes that made up half the fee for leading them safely over the mountains. The rest was due when they crossed into Spain. The Andorran simply shrugged and pocketed the cash, and the Parisian fell silent, wisely deciding to save his energy for the long, gruelling walk to freedom.

Now they were almost there; they had to be. The Parisian stood up, nodded to his wife and son and, with the case still grasped tightly in one hand, walked over to the Andorran, who smiled at him for the first time since their journey had begun, and then pointed in the direction they had been travelling.

"Spain," he said. "Almost in Spain."

The other man nodded, understanding.

"Come, I'll show you where we go next," the Andorran said, striding away and beckoning for him to follow.

The Parisian hesitated for a moment, glanced back at his wife with a look of confusion, and then hurried after the Andorran. He caught up with him, rounding a turn in the narrow path, and they continued for another twenty metres or so to where a small plateau gave a clear view through distant peaks.

The plateau was little more than a ledge with a steep drop down one side to a dense mass of bushes and vegetation far below.

Standing back from the edge, the Andorran pointed into the distance. "There, to the right, the two peaks close together. Through there, that is where we are going."

The Parisian shook his head. "I don't understand. You speak too fast. Speak more slowly."

The Andorran smiled again and gently took the nervous Parisian by the shoulders, manoeuvring him across and in front of him. He leaned down and forward, his cheek close to the other man's and pointed again. "There, follow my arm to where I am pointing. To the right, the two peaks."

Squinting through his gold-rimmed glasses, the Parisian craned forward. "What am I looking at? Is that Spain? Is that where…?"

They were his final words. With incredible speed, the Andorran whipped a long-bladed hunting knife from somewhere in the depths of his sheepskin jerkin, and in one fluent move, pulled back the man's head with his left hand and drew the sharp blade across his throat with his right. Blood spurted in an explosion of crimson as the blade sliced through his windpipe. His legs buckled and the Andorran let him drop to the ground, where he rolled onto his back, choking on his own pumping blood, his eyes staring in disbelief. His body twitched twice.

The Andorran bent down and wiped both sides of the knife's blade on the dead man's raincoat, leaving two bloody streaks. He plucked the gold-rimmed glasses off the staring face and slipped them into a pocket. Then he prised open the dead man's fingers, which were now clasping the handle of the leather case even more tightly. It was locked but the catches were easily forced with the strong blade.

Exactly as he had suspected, there was cash inside. Wads of notes, each neatly folded and secured. He slipped one into a pocket; the rest would be shared later with his companions and the contact who had given them the tip about the fleeing family. There was plenty to go around, especially as the case also contained jewellery: bracelets, necklaces, rings and a carved wooden box containing gold coins.

Grinning at a job well done, the Andorran closed and fastened the case, stood up and, with one foot, pushed the dead man off the edge, watching him tumble over and over, down the steep mountainside and into the vegetation. The body seemed to snag on a branch and was somehow held so that an arm and a leg were still visible. The Andorran sighed. This meant climbing down to free the corpse; they could leave no visible evidence for others passing that way. But then the branch snapped and the body moved again, vanishing from sight, continuing down into the hidden abyss.

All that remained was the man's hat. The Andorran plucked it from the ground and stuffed it into his pocket. It was a good hat; too good to waste.

A sudden anguished scream cut through the air and the Andorran glanced back towards where he had left his friends with the woman and her son. A second scream rang out and the Andorran laughed out loud. This time they were not the screams of a marmot.

ONE

Antwerp, Belgium

War wasn't so bad. Or at least it could have been a lot worse. That was how Paul Hansen saw it. And he wasn't the only one. He had discussed it at school with his friends and at home with his parents. All right, no one actually wanted the Germans here in Antwerp, but here they were and not much could be done about that. Nevertheless, life, in general, wasn't too bad.

The shops still had food. Antwerp was one of the largest ports in Europe and the mighty river Scheldt was still busy with cargo ships coming and going, so the city would always be well supplied. The trains and the trams were still running. Paul still went to school. He could still ride his two-stroke motorcycle over the cobbled streets near his home on the Nationalestraat and all the way down to the docks and the office where his father worked. And when Paul was on the bike, most German soldiers gave him a smile and friendly wave as he went chugging by.

A night-time curfew was in place, but Paul was rarely out

after dark. There was talk of young Belgian men being taken away to Germany to work in munitions factories, but it hadn't happened yet. There was always gossip; it rarely came to anything. Besides, Paul was only sixteen. The talk was of eighteen year olds going. By the time they got around to him, *if* it happened, the war would be over. Everyone said it would.

Paul was on his bike, riding towards his father's office. Edward Hansen was an important man on the docks, a senior manager, responsible for a huge stretch of the waterfront and the hundreds of dockers who worked there.

Dodging the tram rails, Paul guided the motorcycle around the wide Groenplaats, where elderly Belgians and German army officers sat on café terraces, basking in the late afternoon sun. He rode past the towering cathedral and the civic buildings of the Grote Markt and on down to the waterfront, his favourite part of the city.

After less than three years in Antwerp, Paul knew his way around its roads and walkways as well as almost anyone.

Turning northwards, with the Scheldt to his left, he bounced along the cobbled road for half a mile, past huge wharves with forests of towering cranes, glimpsing every so often the bulk of a vessel. Finally he came to a long stretch of iron railings and then a pair of tall gates, which opened into the yard. On the far side, a flight of rickety wooden steps led up to his father's office.

Paul pulled the bike to a sudden standstill as he saw, almost too late, that the gates were closed. Usually they were left open, the yard humming with activity – dockers hurrying everywhere, cranes swinging out over the water and back again, a queue of waiting railway trucks swallowing up the cargo. Now there was no one to be seen. And nothing was moving.

For a moment, Paul was unsure what to do. He cut the bike's engine, climbed off the machine and rested it against the railings. Slowly, he walked to the gates and tried the handle. They were locked.

Glancing around, he realized the street was deserted too, as though everyone had shut themselves away behind closed doors. But he sensed that curious eyes were watching him, peering from shaded windows, waiting to see what he would do.

He looked at his watch. Four forty-five, exactly the time he'd arranged to meet his father. He tried the gate handle again, rattling it noisily, pushing harder this time. But it made no difference.

Paul heard footsteps hurriedly approaching and then felt a strong hand grip one shoulder. "Quiet, Paul," a voice hissed. "You'll bring the Germans if they hear that racket."

Paul turned to see Jos Theys, his father's closest friend. "What's happening?" he asked. "Why is the gate locked, and where is my—?"

"There's no time, Paul. We must get away from here."

"But—"

"Don't argue," Jos snapped. "I'll tell you later. We must go. I've a car nearby."

"But my bike—"

"Leave it!"

Jos yanked the boy's arm, but before they could move they heard shouting from within the yard and saw Edward Hansen run from behind the corrugated tin wall of a warehouse. He was sprinting towards the gates, still fifty metres away.

"Dad!" Paul shouted. "Dad!"

"Get away, Paul!" his father screamed. "Run! Run!"

Paul couldn't move. His feet were rooted to the spot. His father was still thirty metres from the gates when two German soldiers raced from behind the warehouse. One of them raised a submachine-gun.

"Halt!" the soldier yelled. "Halt or I fire!"

But Paul's father didn't stop; he tore desperately onwards.

A single short burst from the weapon knocked the running man off his feet, propelling him forwards even faster for an instant and sending him sprawling. As he hit the ground, a large bunch of keys spilled from his right hand and Paul watched them skid towards the gates and stop a few metres away.

Edward Hansen lay motionless as the two soldiers started to run again, one of them shouting to Paul and Jos.

"You there! Halt!"

Paul was staring at his father's lifeless body as a German officer came into view. He bawled a furious command at the soldiers, who instantly stopped and turned back.

Jos gripped Paul's arm. "Run, Paul! With me, now!"

"But my dad—"

"Now!"

Jos almost pulled Paul off his feet. Suddenly they were running, and Paul found himself being dragged across the road and into one of the many narrow lanes fringing the dockside.

TWO

Paul gazed down from the second-floor window onto the early morning gloom shrouding Sint-Jansplein. A light drizzle fell steadily, turning the cobbles from grey to black. The square was deserted, save for a tram which went clanking and lumbering by.

Everything was strange and unfamiliar. The flat, where he had been hidden for the past fourteen or fifteen hours; the kindly elderly couple who lived there, nodding and smiling sympathetically each time he caught their eyes; the room where he had slept – or not slept; just lain awake for hour after hour turning over in his mind the horror he had witnessed. It all felt unreal.

His father was dead.

At first Paul couldn't believe it; wouldn't believe it. But then the sharp sound of the single blast from the submachine-gun rang through his head and he saw, again, his father motionless on the ground. Over and over he heard the staccato burst and saw him. Dead.

Paul remembered little of running through the dockside streets, being shoved into Jos's car and driven to Sint-Jansplein. Everything was jumbled and confused. And he didn't hear the hurried, murmured conversation that followed between Jos and the elderly couple.

Jos left almost immediately, saying he would be back in the morning to explain as much as he could. Paul was too stunned to argue. He watched him go without a word and then sank down onto the nearest chair.

Three times the elderly couple offered food and drink, and each time Paul refused it. How could he eat when he was filled with fear and worry? Finally he was led to a bedroom at the rear of the flat, where he spent the longest night of his sixteen years; hour after endless hour of tortured thoughts about his father. And his mother... Where was she? Was she safe?

At last, morning arrived, but so far, Jos had not.

The smell of freshly brewed coffee drifted from the kitchen and a few minutes later the door opened. "Would you like coffee?" the woman asked softly. "A little breakfast?"

Paul shook his head. "No, thank you. When will Jos be here?"

The woman shrugged her shoulders. "Soon, I think. My husband says soon."

She smiled and gently closed the door, and Paul turned back to the window. The light was a little stronger, but the rain still fell. One or two people hurried across the square, collars or umbrellas raised. Life went on.

Paul's thoughts turned again to his mother. She would be devastated. His parents were – had been – totally devoted to each other. And she would be frantic with worry about her son, even if Jos had told her he was safe.

Here. In this flat. This strange, unfamiliar flat, with its dark, heavy furniture, its silver-framed, yellowing photographs of stern-looking strangers and its smells of coffee and wax polish.

As raindrops settled on the windowpane, Paul watched them trace a jagged path down the glass. He thought of his parents. He had only properly known them for the past three years.

Before then he was at boarding school in England. His parents were busy criss-crossing Europe, with his father overseeing major improvements to the continent's largest docks. And where Edward Hansen went, his wife, Clarisse, went too. They were inseparable.

Edward Hansen's own mother had been French and his father English, and Paul went to the same boarding school his dad had attended as a boy.

Paul loved every moment of his time in England. He never felt particularly French – or English – or even Belgian, like his mother. Paul was proud of his mixed parentage and his mixed grandparentage. On his father's side there was also a French grandmother, and on his mother's side there was a Belgian grandfather and another French grandmother.

And, like his parents, Paul was naturally good at languages. He spoke English, French and, now, Flemish fluently. Most people hearing him speak in any of the three would assume he was a native.

Which, of course, he was.

There was a soft knock at the front door and the elderly man hurried in from the kitchen.

"Who is it?" he asked.

"It's me, Jos."

The man unlatched the door, pulled it open and Jos Theys, his face drawn and haggard, stepped inside and walked quickly over to Paul. The elderly couple hovered in the background.

There was no time for pleasantries. "You must prepare yourself for more bad news, Paul," Jos said.

"What do you mean?"

"Your mother, she's been taken in by the Germans. Yesterday evening, before I could speak to her."

Paul's heart thudded in his chest. "Taken in? But why? Where?"

"We don't know. But the Germans are looking for you too."

"Why is this happening?" Paul suddenly shouted, leaping to his feet with tears in his eyes. "I don't know what's going on. I don't understand any of it."

"Sit down, Paul," Jos said gently. "I'm going to explain as much as I can. Please sit down."

Paul sank back into his chair, suddenly afraid to hear what Jos was about to tell him.

"Your father was a very brave man," Jos said. "He led our group here in Antwerp. He made operations on the docks as difficult as possible for the Germans by slowing everything down. Little things – freight held up or sent to the wrong destination, cargo not unloaded when or where it should be. It all makes a difference."

"Your group?" Paul asked. "You ... you mean—?"

"Yes, the Resistance movement. Edward started it here. There were just a few of us at first, but the numbers are growing all the time, mainly due to your father's tireless efforts. But someone betrayed him, perhaps one of our own. And that means we're all in danger."

"And my mother ... is she in danger?"

"She was working with us, Paul. Your parents did everything together."

"But why did they kill him?"

"I think it was a mistake," Jos answered with a sigh.

"A mistake?"

Jos nodded. "As we were running away, there was an officer shouting at the soldiers. They stopped chasing us and turned back to your father."

"I don't remember," Paul said, "it was all so quick."

"The officer seemed furious," Jos said. "Your father was

far too important to the Germans to be killed. They wanted to take him alive."

"Then why did they do it?"

"I believe the soldier acted on his own initiative. They didn't expect Edward to grab the keys and make a run for it, and when he didn't stop running, the soldier simply opened fire. He's probably regretting that decision."

"But why was my dad so important to them? Because he formed the Resistance group and could give them names? You just said there may be someone who's already doing exactly that."

"Yes, you're right," Jos said. "But your father had much more important information, vital information that could have a major bearing on the outcome of the entire war."

Paul's eyes widened, his thoughts racing as one stunning revelation followed another. "What information?"

The elderly couple were still nearby, listening but saying nothing. Jos glanced at them and, without a word, they went into the kitchen and shut the door.

Jos leaned closer to Paul and spoke softly. "Over the past few years your father has been responsible for overseeing massive changes to all the largest docks and harbours in Europe, including those in Germany."

"Yes," Paul said, "he told me about them."

"He probably knew more about present-day German harbours than anyone outside Germany; the design, the layout, and even more importantly, the defences and military installations. Just think what the British Government could have done with that information. It could have changed the course of the war."

Paul nodded, anxious for Jos to continue.

"Your father was just about to share that information with the British, but at the last moment someone betrayed him. That's why the Germans acted so quickly and why killing him must have been an error. They needed to find out exactly what he knew and who he might already have talked to."

"Yes," Paul breathed, nodding his head again as the pieces of the puzzle gradually fell into place. "I see that now."

"And as your mother went everywhere with him," Jos went on, "I imagine the Germans will be interrogating her at this very moment. But if I know Clarisse, she'll tell them nothing." He paused for a moment and stared into Paul's eyes. "If they find you, it will be your turn."

"But I don't know anything."

Jos shrugged. "The Germans are unlikely to believe that, which is why we must get you out of Antwerp quickly."

"Get me out? To where?"

"To England."

"But I can't! Not while my mother's—"

"There's nothing you can do for your mother, Paul. Not now. All we can do is wait for information, and hope."

Paul stood up and went to the window, trying to give himself a few moments to collect his thoughts. The rain had stopped; a few more people were milling about the square. On the far side, a baker's shop had opened its doors, and lights burned dimly in the café next door to it.

"How will you get me to England?" Paul asked, turning back to Jos.

"Your family's escape was planned some time ago," Jos replied. "Edward was due to hand the group over to me in the next few days and then all three of you were to leave. It would have meant a new life in England, at least until the war is over."

Paul shook his head. "I had no idea. They never said a word."

"It was for your own safety. Edward could have gone earlier; the British wanted him there, but he refused to leave until he was completely satisfied that the group here in Antwerp could function without him." He paused again, looking at Paul. "He was always stubborn, your father. Perhaps you're like him?"

"I don't know," Paul answered with a shrug. "My mother sometimes says I am."

Jos smiled. "But not too stubborn to see that we have to get you away from here. Your false papers are already prepared."

"Papers? Why do I need false papers if I'm crossing the channel to England?"

"No, that's impossible now," Jos said, shaking his head. "The Germans check every vessel heading out to sea and have every metre of the coastline under surveillance. You'll be taking a much longer, but far safer, route."

Paul sat down again. "I don't understand. Which route?"

"You're travelling south; everything is being arranged," Jos said. "Down through France, across the Pyrenees into Spain, and from there to England. We have contacts in a small town in the south of France. They will be waiting for you and when the time is right, they will organize for you to cross the mountains."

Paul could hardly believe what he was hearing. "Where is this town?"

When Jos replied his voice was little more than a whisper. "It's close to the mountains, in the Ariège region. You'll be safe there until you cross. The town is called..." He glanced at the door to be certain that even the trusted elderly couple would not hear his next word. "...Lavelanet."

THREE

Lavelanet, France

When Henri Mazet was anxious he was in the habit of gently smoothing the left side of his bushy moustache with the index finger of his right hand. It was comforting, reassuring, and so much a part of him that often he didn't even realize he was doing it.

Henri was waiting for his lunch. Three empty soup bowls sat ready to be filled from the pot of vegetable soup, cooling on a place mat on the polished, dark-wood table. His wife, Hélène, sighed as she watched her husband smooth his moustache, knowing that it wasn't the lateness of lunch that was making him anxious, it was the absence of their daughter, Josette.

The clock on the dining-room wall ticked loudly, each passing second seeming to increase Henri's anxiety. And as the minute hand flicked onto twenty past the hour, Henri gave a grunt of exasperation and placed both hands on the table. "One o'clock," he said crossly to his wife. "She knows we have lunch at one o'clock. All she has to do is collect a baguette on her way home. Is that so difficult? Even for her? The soup will be cold by now."

Hélène gave a slight shrug of her shoulders. "I can easily warm it."

"That's not the point. She knows what time we have lunch, so why can't she——?"

Before Henri could finish, they heard the front door swing open and slam shut, followed by footsteps hurrying down the hallway.

"Sorry! Sorry I'm late," Josette said, dropping the still-warm baguette onto the breadboard and dragging a chair from beneath the table. Her dark eyes were bright with excitement.

"One o'clock," her father said, snatching the baguette and sawing at it with the breadknife. "Lunch is always at one o'clock, so why——?"

"I said I'm sorry, Papa," Josette interrupted, settling onto her chair. "I didn't mean to be late, but I stopped at the café and——"

"The café!" Henri growled. "I've told you not to go into that place."

"I didn't go *into* it," Josette said quickly. "I sat on the terrace."

Henri turned to his wife. "What can I do with the girl?" he said, waving the breadknife in the air. "She doesn't listen to a word I tell her."

"I *do* listen, Papa," Josette said. "But Jean-Pierre Dilhat was there, talking to some of his friends. I had to hear what he was saying."

Henri and Hélène exchanged another brief look. "Your father's right," Hélène said. "You shouldn't be in that place."

"But I wasn't in—"

"*Or* on the terrace. It's not right for a girl of your age to be there alone."

"But, Maman, I'm sixteen."

"That's exactly what I mean."

Josette clicked her tongue with irritation. "Maman, you don't understand. Things are changing so fast, we have to know what's going on. And Jean-Pierre says—"

"Jean-Pierre!" Henri snapped. "That young man should keep his thoughts to himself and his mouth shut. He'll get himself into trouble."

"Jean-Pierre isn't afraid of trouble."

"Then he should be!" Henri shouted.

Josette looked stunned. Her father had a loud voice; it was said that all the people of Lavelanet had loud voices because the constant noise of the looms from the town's textile factories had damaged their hearing. Henri ran his own factory, where the din from the machines could be thunderous. But although her father could be irritable, he was generally a kindly, good-hearted man. And he rarely, if ever, shouted.

With a long sigh, Henri finally placed the breadknife back on the table. "Yes, Josette, things are changing, and very quickly." His mind turned back to the tumultuous events of the past few months. After nearly a year of what became known as the "Phoney War", with virtually no fighting on French soil, German forces had suddenly launched their ferocious invasion of France, Belgium and the Netherlands. In less than seven weeks it was all over. The British Expeditionary Force had been evacuated from the beaches at Dunkirk, and the Netherlands, Belgium and, finally, France had surrendered.

Now, the French in both the north and south of the country were adjusting to a new way of life. The north and the entire Atlantic Coast were occupied by German troops, while the south was being governed by a hurriedly set-up French administration based in Vichy.

Henri sighed. "Perhaps we are fortunate that the Germans are busy in the north and have left this part of the country to the new government in Vichy."

"But it's not a real government, Papa; not elected," Josette argued, her eyes dark with defiance. "And Marshal Pétain and the others, they're not real leaders; they're collaborators, puppets of the Nazis."

"Is that what Jean-Pierre says?"

"Yes, it is, but it's what I believe as well."

Henri nodded. "And you think that just because the Germans aren't here in Lavelanet, they don't have people listening out for exactly that kind of talk? It's dangerous, Josette, and you are too trusting and free with your thoughts. Jean-Pierre Dilhat too."

"But we can't do *nothing*," Josette said. "We can't just sit back and let the Germans run the rest of our lives. We have to fight back…" She hesitated for a moment, but could not stop herself. "We should know that better than anyone, Papa!"

The room was suddenly silent save for the ticking clock. Josette glanced over to a silver-framed photograph sitting alone on the sideboard. A young man, bright-eyed, smiling, and dressed in the uniform of the French army, stared proudly out at the camera.

It was the last photograph taken of Josette's brother, Venant, who had been killed fighting for his country just days after the Germans stormed France.

Josette turned to her mother. "I'm sorry, Maman, I shouldn't have said—"

A tear rolled slowly down Hélène Mazet's face and she wiped it away with the sleeve of her black cardigan. Since her son's death she wore black every day, and she cried every night.

She stood up and took the pot from the table with both hands. "I'll warm the soup."

"I don't want any," Henri said in a hoarse whisper.

Josette watched as her mother walked silently from the room. Then she looked at the photograph of her brother again, her own eyes moistening, before turning to her father. He was staring down at the table, his chin propped on his right hand, as his finger rhythmically smoothed the bristles of his moustache.

FOUR

The barge, *Marina*, secured forward and aft, rested low in the murky brown waters of the Scheldt. She was fully laden with coal and sitting so heavily that the swiftly flowing tidal river was almost washing over her sides.

Paul gazed at the barge from the passenger seat of Jos's car. The snub-nosed, tar-black vessel must have been well over thirty metres long and five wide. Towards the stern, a square wheelhouse perched above what, Paul guessed, was the living area, with small, curtained windows looking forward and to both sides. Behind the wheelhouse, two bicycles stood upright in a large wooden stand, and from a pole at the stern, the Belgian flag, with its vertical stripes of black, yellow and red, flew proudly in the stiff breeze.

Jos had been on board the barge for a few minutes, having told Paul to wait while he checked that all was ready. They were well away from the main sprawl of Antwerp's massive dock complex, with its forests of masts and funnels and cranes, and the areas where barges sat roped side by side, awaiting their turn to be loaded or unloaded. Here it was quiet; the *Marina* lay alongside a small, empty wharf that appeared to have fallen into disrepair. Jos's car was parked between the water and the rusting wharf building, hidden from the road and any inquisitive passing dock-worker or German army patrol.

In the back of the vehicle was a small suitcase containing a couple of changes of clothes Jos had managed to find from somewhere. And in an inside pocket of Paul's jacket were his new papers, his identity card and travel visa – both expertly forged. Jos had told him these were for future use, once he was travelling openly in France. But his dangerous journey south was to begin with being smuggled through Belgium on board the *Marina*.

If he had been thinking clearly, Paul would have been surprised when Jos said his journey to southern France was to start on a river barge going inland, deeper into Belgium and towards Germany. But Paul was still too shocked at his father's death and the revelations that followed. He merely nodded when Jos told him that the roads and railways out of the city were too closely guarded and that the slower route, by barge, was by far the safest one.

As Paul watched, Jos emerged from the *Marina*'s wheel-house, glanced around and then hurried down the gangplank and over to the car. He got inside and closed the door quietly. "Everything is ready. Albert is waiting for you."

Paul stared at the *Marina*. "Why are there two bicycles

on the back of the boat – is someone else onboard?"

"I asked Albert the same question," Jos answered, his eyes shifting to the black bicycles standing upright, like guards, at the back of the vessel. "There was a young man working with him on the barge, a Belgian Jew. The second bike is his. When the Germans invaded he got scared. He disappeared and didn't return when they were due to start the last voyage. Albert says he's keeping the bike there just in case he turns up."

Paul glanced at the bicycles again, trying to picture the young man and imagine his terror as the Germans advanced on Antwerp. The realities of the war were hitting home one after another. He sighed and reached for the door handle, but Jos put a hand out to stop him. "Paul," he said, "a moment."

"Yes?" Paul said.

"Before you leave, I must ask you once more, are you certain you know nothing about our group here in Antwerp or about the German ports your father visited?"

"I told you before," Paul said. "Nothing."

"Yes, but now you've had time to think?"

"Still nothing."

"Are you certain?" Jos persisted. "Absolutely certain?"

"Yes," Paul said, a little irritably. "I don't know anything about the Resistance or about my dad's visits. Only that he worked at harbours in Germany, and other places too."

Eyes narrowing and voice hardening, Jos pressed on.

"But he must have told you something about those visits? Try to remember."

"I can't."

"Then try harder. What exactly did he tell you, Paul? What did he say about the port of Hamburg, for instance?"

Paul was tired. He'd spent a sleepless night and his mind was still trying to come to terms with all he had witnessed and heard in the past twenty-four hours. Suddenly he snapped, his eyes flashing angrily, his voice exploding with an angry torrent of words. "How many times do I have to tell you? I know nothing! Nothing! Nothing at all! Understand? My father never told me anything about Hamburg, or—"

Jos loosened his grip on Paul's arm. "It's all right, Paul," he said gently. "It's all right."

The air inside the car was stifling and Paul realized that he was trembling, panting as though he'd been sprinting and was out of breath. He was fit and strong and a keen sportsman. He'd played rugby for his school team in England and football since he'd been in Belgium, and he was an excellent middle-distance runner. But at that moment he felt drained and exhausted.

Jos could see the confusion in his eyes. "You've had a terrible shock, Paul," he said softly. "We needed to let the tension out."

"Is … is that why…?"

"Why I pushed you so hard?" Jos said. He gave a slight smile and nodded. "Partly, but also to remind you that my questions will be nothing compared to what the Germans will do if you're captured. That's why we have to get you to freedom."

They sat in silence for a couple of minutes as Paul's breathing returned to normal and his temper cooled. He felt better, not like his old self, but a bit stronger and more in control of his emotions.

He turned to Jos. "I'm ready."

Jos reached into the back seat to fetch his suitcase, and they stepped from the car and walked quickly to the barge and up the short wooden gangplank. Jos opened the wheelhouse door and led the way down the steep steps into the cabin. "Watch your head," he warned.

Paul was tall for his age, almost as tall as Jos. He had to duck as he followed Jos down the steps. Once in the living quarters, he was surprised by how much headroom and space there was. And heat.

Across the room, resting on the oak floorboards, was a cast-iron, pot-bellied stove, its chimney disappearing through the cabin roof. A large, long-handled pan sat on one of the two cooking plates, and peering into the pan was a giant, bearded man, a few years older than his dad, Paul guessed, and as pot-bellied as the stove itself.

The comforting aroma of simmering food filled the cabin. The man now placed a lid on the pan, looked up, and in just four steps crossed the ancient timbers and held out his right hand to Paul. "Albert," he said, his voice deep and resonant.

Paul's own hand was engulfed in the large fist. "Paul," he said, nodding.

"And that," said Albert, gesturing with his head to a large high-backed chair on the other side of the stove, "is the real master of the *Marina*. Say hello to Baron."

Paul looked over at the chair. At first glance, in the relative gloom of the cabin, the huge shape on the wooden seat might have been an overstuffed cushion. But as his eyes adjusted to the light, he saw the massive, sprawling tabby cat. Two emotionless, yellow-tinted eyes watched Paul carefully, but Baron didn't move a muscle.

For the first time in more than two days, Paul felt himself smile slightly. "Hello, Baron," he said.

Baron stared for a moment, then hauled himself up, gave a great yawn and arched his broad back. He tipped himself forward and landed with a thud before padding over to Paul and nuzzling his head against the boy's trouser leg.

Paul reached down to stroke the cat behind one ear and down his thick, fleshy neck. A loud purr of contentment emerged from somewhere deep in Baron's throat.

"That's good," Albert said, with a laugh. "Baron likes you. And Baron likes very few people. It seems you have a new friend."

"Paul needs friends at the moment." Jos smiled. He glanced at his wristwatch, obviously ready to take his leave and go ashore. He was still holding the small suitcase, which he rested on the chair.

Quick as lightning, Baron's great head whipped around and he hissed fiercely, his yellow eyes glaring.

"What did I do?" Jos gasped.

"That's Baron's chair," Albert said belatedly, "I should have warned you. No one or nothing takes Baron's chair."

Jos snatched the case and held it between himself and the cat. "I apologize, Baron," he said quickly. "I didn't know." Hesitantly he moved to stroke the huge tabby, but a low snarl quickly changed his mind and he took a backward step.

Albert grinned. "As I said, he likes very few people."

"Yes, I see what you mean." Jos placed the suitcase carefully on the floor. "Goodbye then, Paul. I'll try to get news of your mother to you when you reach—" He stopped, avoiding mention of the town Paul was travelling to. "When you reach your destination."

"You're not staying to eat?" Albert asked.

"Eat?" Jos said, surprise registering on his face.

"Of course."

"Is there time? Shouldn't you be getting under way?"

Albert grunted. "There is always time to eat. I must eat, and so must Baron." He nodded towards Paul. "And he looks as if he needs a good meal."

"Then I'll leave you to your food," Jos said. He shook Paul's hand before turning back to Albert. "Thank you for this. You're doing a great service to Belgium and the cause of freedom."

Albert shrugged his bulky shoulders and lifted the lid off

the pan. "You'll regret not staying. It's chicken, like my mother used to make."

"I'm sure it's delicious," Jos replied, smiling, "but I must get back to work." Halfway up the steps he stopped and looked back at Paul. "Good luck, Paul, I'll be thinking of you, and I hope we'll meet again one day." His eyes shifted to Baron, who was padding back towards his chair. "And I'm very sorry, Baron, I hope you can forgive me."

Baron ignored the offered apology, launched himself up onto his chair and settled down to sleep.

Jos continued up the steps and out onto the deck. They heard his footsteps crossing the heavy planks and Paul watched through one of the small windows while he got into his car and drove away.

As the vehicle disappeared behind the rusting wharf, Paul suddenly felt lost and abandoned, stranded on board a tar-soaked barge with an eccentric skipper and a temperamental cat for company.

"It will get easier, I promise you," Albert said. "And Baron and I will do everything we can to help get you to safety. You have my word on that."

The huge man looked down into the cooking pot and gave the chicken a stir with a wooden spoon. "It's ready," he smiled, "and falling off the bone. Maybe not quite as good as my mother's, but almost."

He glanced at Paul. "So, let's eat."

FIVE

lbert was as good as his word. Over the following three
days he went about his work on the *Marina* quietly and
efficiently, making the job of piloting the lumbering vessel
from river to canal look easy, and always finding time to
keep a watchful and reassuring eye on the newest member
of his crew.

While the *Marina* remained on the Scheldt, Paul stayed
below decks, hidden from view. Sleek, grey German patrol
boats prowled the wide harbour waters, their heavily armed
crews challenging, and sometimes boarding, any sea-bound
vessels arousing their suspicion. But the *Marina* was jour-
neying inland so was largely ignored, and once she moved
to the calm of the recently opened canal linking the Scheldt
and Meuse rivers, it became safer for Paul to move about
the barge more freely.

At night he slept fitfully, plagued by dreams of the death
of his father and the arrest of his mother, but in his waking
hours the despair and sense of loss was gradually joined by a

feeling of immense pride. His parents were heroes, both of them, brave and strong, and although Paul continued to mourn his father and fear for his mother, he grew more and more determined to be equally brave and strong. And he made a silent vow to continue to fight the enemy, in whatever way he could. He had to, for his parents. He owed it to them.

There was plenty of time for Paul to think as the *Marina* nosed sedately onwards – perhaps too much. Albert tried to keep him busy, sometimes allowing him to take the wheel on the narrow, straight waters of the canal. In the evenings, with the vessel tied up, he would haul vast amounts of food from his cold store and cook excellent meals, while sinking a couple of bottles of his favourite Belgian beer and regaling Paul with tales of the many cargoes the *Marina* had shifted over the years – both legal and illegal.

"A little smuggling is one of the perks of the business," he told Paul on the second night. "And despite this war, there's still a market for whatever I bring back to Antwerp. German wine has always been popular. Can't stand the stuff myself – give me a good Belgian beer any day – but the rich seem to enjoy it."

"Perhaps they'll like German wine less now we're at war," Paul answered.

Albert took a long drink of beer. "Well, here's two promises, Paul. One, the Germans will never stop me smuggling and, two, we'll drive them out of Antwerp eventually. You mark my words."

Baron also seemed to be looking out for Paul. When the *Marina* was at the canal side, the big tabby was usually stretched out on his chair, half-closed eyes focused on his new friend. And when the barge was nosing through the water and Paul was on deck, Baron often lazed nearby.

At least once a day, though, Baron would disappear down into the gloom of the cargo hold, where almost a thousand tons of coal rested in the darkness like a glistening subterranean mountain range. When he reappeared, coal-dusty but triumphant, the lifeless body of a large brown rat would usually be clenched between his powerful jaws. He would pad along the deck and proudly drop his kill at Paul's feet, before sitting and waiting for a congratulatory stroke behind the ears, which would set him purring loudly.

The countryside appeared peaceful but occasionally they would pass a building shattered by shellfire, a bullet-riddled vehicle, or woodland laid flat by tanks, all evidence of the German army's swift and devastating invasion.

Each graphic sight only increased Paul's determination to be part of the fight back. He knew he would have to wait. For now, he could only go along with the plan to get him to freedom. But later, after he reached England, and as soon as he was old enough, he would volunteer to go into action.

The taking of Antwerp by the Germans had been bloodless; Belgium had surrendered by the time the first enemy troops marched triumphantly up the Keyserlei. And Paul had been there, watching silently with his father, never dreaming of the devastating turn his life would so quickly take. Now his eyes were finally open to the grim reality of war.

As the *Marina* journeyed slowly on, Albert remained ever watchful and ever cautious. Paul's belongings were stowed in a secret hideaway beneath the planks of the cabin, a space usually reserved for smuggled items. As soon as each meal was eaten, the plates and cutlery were washed and stowed, clearing away the evidence of an additional person on board. He had also given Paul precise orders on what to do in an emergency. The moment he caught sight of a barge travelling in the opposite direction he would order Paul below. There would almost certainly be no danger from a fellow bargeman, but these were strange times, he said, so it would be foolish and possibly fatal to take the slightest risk.

Heavy rain was falling as Albert glanced through the back window of the wheelhouse at another barge moving slowly away into the distance. "It's all right, Paul, you can come out now."

Paul climbed up from the cabin, carrying two tin mugs of hot coffee. He placed them on the wide shelf above the *Marina*'s wheel and looked back through the rain towards the retreating barge. "Do you know him?"

Albert nodded. "Old Donald Van de Brul, returning from Germany. Gave me a wave and shouted something, but I didn't want to go out on deck in this rain." He grinned. "Old Donald is always complaining about something. He planned to retire this year, but the Germans will keep him working."

Van de Brul's barge finally disappeared from sight and Paul turned to Albert. "And what about me, where exactly am I going? I still don't know."

"You'll find out soon enough. But I'm sad to say you'll be leaving Baron and me before the end of the voyage."

"Where does the voyage end?"

Albert's face darkened. "When we reach the Meuse, I must turn north towards the Rhine and Germany. This good Belgian coal, cut from the ground by good Belgian hands, is going to German factories to fire the furnaces to make more steel for more weapons."

The weather was darkening with Albert's mood. Low clouds moved swiftly in a strengthening wind, and the rain grew even heavier, thudding against the wheelhouse windows.

The canal was choppy now, with small, white-topped waves spreading across the surface. The *Marina* rose and fell as she ploughed forward, fine spray bouncing off her bows and flying back over the hold covers to splatter against the wheelhouse.

Albert grasped his coffee and took a long drink as he gazed ahead through the smeared glass of the wheelhouse windows. The rain was getting stronger. He wiped his eyes and craned his neck, cursing quietly as he strained to see.

Suddenly he banged the tin mug down on the shelf. "Stupid! I'm so bloody stupid! *That*'s what Donald was trying to tell me!"

"What? What is it?"

"Up ahead, look! Germans! On the bank, an armoured car and soldiers. Go to the hold, Paul! *Go!*"

SIX

The tools stacked and hung on the shelves and walls of Didier Brunet's workshop looked like medieval instruments of torture – heavy chains to shackle some hapless victim, huge metal tongs to prize apart a shattered ribcage, and an array of lethal blades, spikes, spanners and hooks to complete the gruesome business of quartering a body and ripping out its entrails.

They made a terrifying display, but were in fact the innocent tools of Didier's trade, the means by which he kept the heavy but delicate machines of Henri Mazet's textile factory in Lavelanet running smoothly. And Didier was determined that it would continue to run smoothly; he still had much to prove.

Sitting at a wooden bench in the workshop, greasing the spindle of a weighty iron clamp, he listened to the sounds and rhythms of the machines. Each area of the factory floor had its own particular tune, like the different sections of an orchestra. The *cha-kah-dun* of the wool separators, the *ta-ta-ta-psssh* of the spinning looms, the *da-da-doom* of the bobbin winders. Combined and constantly singing, the machines created a deafening cacophony for any visitor. But after four years, Didier could tell instantly when one of his beloved machines was out of tune or even slightly off-key.

Didier had joined Mazet's factory when he left school, just after his fourteenth birthday. Virtually everyone in Lavelanet worked in either the textiles or comb-making industries; there was little else.

And Didier had struck lucky. The long-serving mechanic, Jacques Savary, wanted an apprentice he could train up to take over when he retired a few years later. Didier had impressed him from day one. Jacques spotted straight away that the youngster was a natural with anything mechanical.

"You must have been born with a spanner in your hand," he joked one morning as he watched Didier grease and then free a particularly stubborn bolt from a jammed loom cylinder. "You'll do just fine, boy."

While many of the heavy machines in Mazet's factory were relatively new, some had been built thirty or more years before – built to last. But their solid, cast-iron frames often housed surprisingly intricate and complex moving parts. Wheels, spindles, cylinders, drive belts, shafts; all had to be carefully watched, nurtured and maintained, and Didier grew to recognize each individual machine's peculiarities and particular needs.

He had worked happily with Jacques for three and a half

years, but for the past six months the older man had been unwell. He had struggled bravely on until, three months earlier, he had been ordered by the doctor to take time off and rest. He was unlikely to return.

Didier had been put in charge, temporarily, of the machines. He was young for such a responsibility, but Mazet told him that if, after six months, there had been no major mishaps, then the job would be his permanently. That was assuming Jacques did not come back.

But there was another reason why Didier was doing his utmost to ensure the machines remained in perfect running order and create a good impression with his boss – Henri Mazet's daughter, Josette.

Didier and Josette had known one another since they were children. In a town of five thousand people most of the inhabitants knew one another, by sight at least. During their school days, Didier had paid little attention to Josette, but since she had come to work in the factory, helping her father in the office, he had seen her differently. She was beautiful: long, dark, wavy hair; even darker eyes; a sweet face that could turn fiery in an instant – and frequently did. Didier often found himself sighing and unable to concentrate on his work when he caught sight of Josette.

And from the sighs and embarrassed looks, and the way he became strangely tongue-tied and unsure of what to say, Josette soon realized how Didier felt about her.

"Didier?"

The iron clamp almost fell from Didier's hands as he heard her voice above the machines. He spun around.

She was standing in the doorway. She smiled when she spotted Didier's embarrassed look. She couldn't resist teasing him now, as she often did. "Why are you sitting there with your mouth open? You look like a drowned fish."

Didier closed his mouth and tried to think of what to say.

"My father wants to see you."

Didier nodded; the right words still hadn't come.

"Don't you want to know why?"

Didier swallowed. "Why?"

Josette shrugged her shoulders. "He didn't say."

"I … I … I…"

"What, Didier? What are you trying to say?" Josette gave an innocent smile, knowing exactly the effect her presence had on him.

Didier took a deep breath and the words he had been trying to perfect for more than a fortnight came tumbling from his mouth. "I wondered if you would like to come out with me on Sunday? We could go for a ride on the bike." Didier's proudest possession was his motorbike. "I'll ask your father's permission, of course."

Josette laughed. "Permission?" she said, teasing. "But you're not asking to marry me."

Didier's eyes widened, but he didn't reply. He was lost for words again.

"I don't have to ask Papa's permission for everything I do."

"But I will still ask," Didier said hoarsely, managing to find his voice. "It's only right."

"Please yourself," Josette said with a shrug. "You can ask his permission, but I may be busy on Sunday."

Didier felt his heart sink. "Busy? Where?"

After a quick look behind her to ensure no one was listening, Josette took a step into the workshop. She spoke quietly. "I may be with other friends."

"Which friends?"

Josette stole another look onto the factory floor and then, in little more than a whisper said, "I've heard there may be a meeting, Jean-Pierre Dilhat and others. I want to get involved; be part of it."

"Involved!" Didier said loudly, leaping to his feet, unable to hide his concern.

"Ssshhhh!"

"What do you mean, 'involved'?"

"Oh, don't you start," Josette hissed. "It's bad enough having Papa telling me not to do anything."

"Did Dilhat tell you about this meeting himself?"

"No," Josette answered sheepishly, her face dropping. "I've never actually spoken to him. But I've heard him speak. He's wonderful; we need people like him, to save France."

"And the meeting," Didier said, suddenly more confident, "is it for real? Have you been invited?"

Josette shook her head. "I don't know if it's really

happening or if it's just a rumour. So many people are saying so many different things."

"Then don't listen to them," Didier snapped. "And be careful of what *you* say too. You don't know who you can trust these days."

Josette sighed. "You sound just like my father."

SEVEN

Steam rose from the German officer's greatcoat as he stepped into the wheelhouse, wiping the raindrops from his spectacles with a clean white handkerchief. It was sweltering inside, the heat rising up through the open doorway from the cabin, where the pot-bellied stove burned as usual.

The officer replaced his glasses, slowly and deliberately folded the handkerchief and returned it to his pocket, all the time resting his eyes on Albert, who was leaning against the wheel.

"We are searching for a runaway boy."

Albert said nothing.

"He is aged sixteen and from Antwerp."

Albert shrugged his bulky shoulders. "This is a working barge, no place for boys."

"Let me see your papers."

As Albert turned to reach for his own and the *Marina*'s documents, he spotted the two tin mugs on the shelf. He cursed silently and, as he turned back to the officer, quickly shifted his body to hide the mugs from view.

The officer began to leaf through the papers. Two more soldiers stood nearby, each holding a rifle; another waited on deck, his shoulders hunched against the pounding rain.

"If you refuse to cooperate, I will have you arrested and this old tub impounded, you realize that, don't you?" the officer said, without looking up.

"That wouldn't please the authorities in Berlin," Albert replied. "The coal I'm carrying is going to German factories, as you'll see if you turn to the next page."

The German read quickly and thrust the papers back into Albert's hands. "We received information that the boy escaped on a barge," he said. Then he gestured to the two soldiers. "Search thoroughly."

The two men hurried down the stairs into the living quarters. The officer moved closer until he was standing next to Albert, looking through the window down the length of the *Marina*. Albert could feel perspiration beginning to break out on his brow. If the German were to glance even slightly to his left he would instantly spot the two mugs.

Slowly Albert moved so that he too was looking straight ahead, raising his left arm to hide the mugs. "There are a lot of barges on Belgian waters, you know. Searching them all could take some time." He gestured towards the side window. "Your soldier out there is getting very wet, poor fellow. You can invite him in, I don't mind."

The officer looked at the soldier, instead of the mugs.

"This is not a social visit and our men are trained to endure far worse than a few raindrops."

Albert shrugged. "He doesn't seem very happy."

"There is a bicycle outside on deck," the officer snapped. "In a stand."

"I made it myself. Not beautiful, I know, but it works."

"The stand is for two bicycles, yet I see only one."

"You are very observant," Albert answered.

"So where is the other bicycle?"

Albert smiled and spoke softly. "Between you and me, there is no other bicycle. The other side of the stand is used by my girlfriends."

"Girlfriends?" the officer replied, looking Albert in the eye.

"I travel a long way in this barge," Albert said. "I have girlfriends in certain towns along the rivers and canals. Sometimes they come to visit me."

The officer scowled. "On their bicycles?"

Albert nodded. "On their bicycles. Not all at the same time, of course."

"And you expect me to believe that?"

The smile on Albert's face widened and he winked. "You know what they say about women liking sailors? Well, it's perfectly true."

The officer did not return the smile, but instead glared down into the cabin. The infantrymen were shifting furniture and bunks, and opening and rummaging through cupboards and lockers. They had failed to discover the secret compartment beneath the floorboards.

Eventually they trudged back up the steps. "Nothing, sir," announced the first of them to emerge into the light.

"Then search the cargo holds. And take Schumann with you."

"There's nothing down there but coal," Albert said.

"We shall see about that," the officer replied coldly.

Paul heard the movement, the shifting and sliding of coal, as the three soldiers dropped one after the other from the ladder onto the treacherous black surface. They were near the stern, but in the vast, cavernous space the slightest sound travelled freely, echoing from the damp sides of the vessel.

Albert and Paul had acted swiftly once they spotted the Germans on the canal side, instantly swinging into the emergency plan. While Albert brought the *Marina* to a standstill in mid canal, Paul rushed down into the hold and ran as quickly as he could across the shifting coal to the shallow pit they had dug out before the voyage.

After jumping into the pit, Paul began to cover himself with the coal stacked on either side. A clean sack lay close by and when Albert arrived to complete the operation, Paul's body was almost buried. He watched his young friend sink back into the dusty blackness, turn his head to one side and place a hand against his face, covering his nose and mouth. Albert took the sack, rested it over Paul's head and upper torso and covered it carefully in coal. Within seconds Paul was totally buried. "Stay strong," muttered Albert, leaning close before hurrying back to the wheelhouse.

Now Paul lay in suffocating heat and coffin-like darkness, listening to the German soldiers moving towards him. They had flicked on powerful torches and fixed bayonets to their rifles.

Slowly, they edged closer, their boots slipping on the uneven surface. After every few paces they prodded their bayonets into the coal. Paul heard muffled voices and glimpsed flashes of brilliant light as the torch beams bounced from the coal onto the *Marina*'s tar-drenched sides.

The heat was stifling. Paul's muscles were stiffening through lack of movement. But he remained absolutely still, refusing to allow himself to shift even one centimetre. The slightest movement could start a coal slide and give away his hiding place. He could hear his own breathing slowing, becoming shallower.

The soldiers came nearer, their boots sounding heavier, their voices louder, still thrusting their bayonets into the coal after every few steps.

Paul's cramped muscles felt as if they were screaming in agony. He could taste coal dust in his throat and mouth; worse, it was clogging his nose, making it more and more difficult to breathe. And the heat was almost unbearable. He was desperate to cough, or sneeze.

And then, despite himself, he did. One small, half-choked sneeze escaped from his nose and mouth, and his entire body jerked slightly. It was enough to cause lumps of coal to tumble away from his hiding place, like a small landslip on a ski slope.

He froze.

The three soldiers froze.

The hold was totally silent.

Seconds passed. Four. Five. More. Terrifying seconds of silence. Paul could do nothing but hold his breath and focus on Albert's words: *Stay strong. Stay strong.*

Then the Germans began to speak, almost in whispers, as though they were somehow afraid of the sound they had heard.

"You heard it too?"

"Over there, on the right."

Flashes of light darted and danced above Paul as he lay completely still, dreading that the tumbling coal had revealed part of his body or the sack covering his head.

"Go over, take a look."

One soldier took a hesitant step forward. And then a second step, and a third.

Suddenly there was another sound; another sneeze, but much louder.

The soldiers froze again.

"What the—?"

"What's going on?"

"Look, there, over there. No, in my torchlight! There!"

The light flicked away from Paul, plunging him back into darkness.

And then, unbelievably, he heard the Germans laughing.

All three soldiers were laughing. And then one of them started to clap his hands. He was applauding.

"Look at the size of that rat."

"And the cat! He's bigger than our dog back home."

"He's bringing it to you, Kurt. Look, he's bringing you a present."

"Thank you, thank you, my friend. Yes, you're very clever. And you look very pleased with yourself."

There was more laughter and Paul heard the soldiers speaking again.

"So what are you going to do with your gift, Kurt?"

"Maybe I should give it to Hauptmann Mueller; might cheer him up."

"Huh! Nothing's going to make Mueller smile until we find the kid."

"Well, there's nothing down here but a dead rat and a cat that's bigger than my dog. Come on, let's get out. Hauptmann's information must be wrong. Maybe the kid escaped by bike."

Footsteps sounded. They were moving away, back up the ladder towards daylight.

A long, slow breath emerged from deep within Paul's body and, at last, he allowed himself to breathe.

EIGHT

"**D**idn't I tell you? Baron is the most intelligent cat I have ever encountered. His brain is much bigger than mine – but, then, it's not difficult for a cat to have a bigger brain than mine." Albert laughed, from relief as much as at his own joke. "He deserves a medal!"

Albert was calling down from the wheelhouse to the cabin, where Paul had been washing away the visible traces of his terrifying time in the cargo hold. He coughed for what felt like the hundredth time. His mouth, his nose, his throat, his entire body still felt thick with coal dust.

"He probably saved our lives, Paul," Albert went on. "Both of us. You realize that, don't you?"

Paul coughed again as he continued towelling his hair dry. He grinned at Baron, who was sprawled on his chair, taking no notice of the praise being lavished upon him.

"How are you feeling now?" Albert called.

"I'm fine," Paul managed to say, before sneezing loudly, which seemed at last to clear his nose. He threw down the towel, walked over to Baron and stroked him behind the ears.

"Thank you," Paul said softly. "You are a hero."

Baron purred.

"Is it all right if I come up?" Paul called from the bottom of the cabin steps after a couple of minutes.

"Yes, we're safe for the moment."

Once back in the wheelhouse, Paul went straight to the deck door, pulled it open and gulped the fresh air. The rain had stopped and the *Marina* was pushing steadily on through calmer waters.

"An hour more and we'll stop for the night," Albert said. "I can't tell you how much I'm looking forward to my first beer. You know, we almost gave the game away ourselves."

"How?" Paul asked, closing the door and moving to join Albert at the wheel.

"Our two coffee mugs were sitting on the shelf there. I managed to hide them from that smug officer just in time."

"Lucky."

"Not luck, Paul, it took skill and nerve. Nerves of steel, I have." He laughed. "And it was a good idea to leave the other bike back in Antwerp, eh?"

"A very good idea," Paul agreed. "Now the Germans are out there somewhere searching for a boy on a bicycle."

"You should have seen the officer's face when his men told him about Baron and the rat. He couldn't get ashore quick enough."

Paul stared through the window towards the darkening

horizon. He was buzzing with excitement, elated that they had succeeded in outwitting the Germans. But there was a nagging worry. "How did they know I was on a barge?"

"I've been wondering about that myself," Albert said. "I suppose it's like Jos Theys says, there must be someone in Antwerp betraying the whole set-up. The bastard."

They stood in silence for a few moments, each deep in his own thoughts.

Finally Albert broke the silence. "The Germans didn't know *which* barge though. The officer just said they had information that you were were escaping on a barge. But then, perhaps…"

"What?" Paul asked.

Albert shook his head. "Nothing, just my stupid thoughts leading nowhere. You're in real danger, that's for sure. But after tomorrow perhaps you'll be in a little less danger."

Before Paul could reply, Albert pointed ahead. Another barge was approaching from the opposite direction. It was a good hundred metres away, but Albert was taking no chances. "I never got to finish my coffee, and neither did you. How about you go and brew some more?"

Paul nodded and went below. By the time he returned, the other barge had long passed.

Albert sipped the hot coffee from the tin mug, knowing that Paul was waiting for him to speak. "Tomorrow you leave me, Paul. I was going to tell you tonight, but it's only fair that you know now."

The news was unsettling for Paul, as he was just getting accustomed to life on board the *Marina*. "I've liked being with you," he said. "And Baron."

Paul saw that his words had pleased Albert. But the bargeman's eyes hardened almost instantly. "In these uncertain times, it's probably safest and wisest not to become too attached to anyone." He paused to let his words sink in. "On the *Marina* you're virtually a sitting target; at best a very slow-moving target. If there is, as Jos suspects, a traitor in Antwerp, we've been making it easy for him."

"Or her?" Paul said.

"Yes, that's possible," Albert answered with a shrug. "From tomorrow you become more difficult to trace, especially when you leave Belgium, away from the control of Antwerp. And even though the Resistance movement isn't fully organized, there are already a few rules. One of those rules is that when we're moving someone, someone like you, each of us knows only the next person in the chain. On either side, of course."

Paul's brow creased. "I don't quite understand."

"It's like this," Albert said. "I know only Jos and the person I pass you on to. That person knows only me, and the person he passes you on to. And so on. Everyone knows who they need to know, and what they need to know, and nothing else. You see?"

"Yes," Paul said. "But surely back in Antwerp they know everyone in the chain?"

Albert shook his head. "No, in Antwerp they know your ultimate destination but not exactly who you're travelling with, or the route. That's left to the contacts on the ground. It has to be; they know the area and the potential dangers. And it's much safer that way. If someone in the chain is taken by the enemy, they can't reveal what they don't know."

Albert took another sip of coffee and then spat it back into the mug. "I know one thing; I've had enough of this stuff. I need a beer."

NINE

Rivel was just eighteen kilometres from Lavelanet. Approached along a road flanked on either side by lines of plane trees, it was quiet and unremarkable.

In the summer months, villagers would be out early, walking to one or other of the two shops, or perhaps both, or tending patches of garden, with their crops of leeks and garlic, peppers and tomatoes. By the middle of the day, when the sun was at its strongest, the shutters on the windows would be pulled to and the few narrow streets would be deserted, the inhabitants of Rivel lingering within the cool stone walls of their houses, waiting for the heat to pass.

Rivel was like many other sleepy southern French villages – save for one thing. On its outskirts, just away from the muddle of streets and alleyways and houses, on the road leading to the nearby town of Chalabre, was a camp. Four long, low buildings sat in an open area surrounded on all sides by a high barbed-wire fence. And there, around two hundred and fifty prisoners waited anxiously to discover their fate.

Didier Brunet had pulled his motorbike off the road into the shade of the trees. He stood in the shadows, hidden from the road and the eyes of the guards, less than a hundred metres away. Josette was at his side. They watched the prisoners, dressed in dull brown uniforms, walking lethargically in circles around the open area. More were inside the long huts, doing what they could to avoid the baking sun.

"Who are they?" Josette asked, peering towards the camp.

"Many of them are Germans," Didier replied.

Josette wheeled around, her eyes flashing. "If that's supposed to be a joke, then it's not funny."

"Calm down," Didier said quietly. "It's not a joke; it's true."

"But how can they be Germans?"

Didier gestured for Josette to follow him and they walked a little further from the road and sat at the base of a tree. "They're Germans and Austrians who were living in France when the war started. The government thought they might be spies for the Nazis, so they rounded them up and put them in camps like this one."

"Then why haven't they been released? The Germans rule us now."

"It's not quite as simple as that," Didier answered. "The new government and their German friends have decided that because these men were living in France before the war, they might be *anti*-Nazi in fact. So they have to stay in prison."

"But that's crazy."

"This whole war is crazy."

Didier leaned against the tree, tilting his head back so that the warmth of the sun touched his face. "And things have changed recently. It's no longer just Germans and Austrians inside the camps, it's Frenchmen too."

"Who are they? Criminals?"

"Our new government and the Nazis would tell you they're criminals," Didier replied with a short laugh. "In reality it's anyone they think might possibly cause them a problem. Democrats, trade unionists, communists, anyone suspected of being involved in any sort of protest or resistance." He lowered his head, out of the sunlight, and the shadows gave a serious and worried look to his usually bright face. "That's why you have to be careful; it won't only be men they put in these camps."

Josette breathed hard. "Is that why you brought me here?"

"I brought you here to show you what's happening in our country. And to remind you that you're playing with fire if you get too close to people like Jean-Pierre Dilhat."

"Jean-Pierre is a patriot!" Josette snapped.

"Oh, yes, he's a patriot all right," Didier snapped back, "I don't doubt that. But he's a fool if he goes around talking about it constantly."

"Someone has to bring people together to fight back."

"Oh, Josette, you are so naive!"

They were both almost shouting. Josette stood up and

started walking towards the motorbike. "Better than doing nothing, or just sitting back and waiting for someone else to act for you. And, anyway, why do you care?"

Didier leapt to his feet. "Because…"

Josette stopped and turned back. "Yes?"

After all his earlier confidence, Didier was tongue-tied again. "Because…"

"Because what?"

They stared at each other, Josette silently challenging Didier to answer.

Finally he did. "You … you know I … I like you."

Suddenly Josette felt terribly guilty. She'd teased and taunted Didier again and she knew it wasn't fair. "I … I'm sorry, Didier."

"What for?"

Now it was Josette's turn to be lost for words. "I … I…"

"Come on, say what you have to say."

"I like you too, Didier, but…" Her voice trailed away.

"You don't want me as a boyfriend," Didier said. "Is that it?"

Josette looked at the ground, but nodded her head.

"Is there someone you prefer?"

"No," Josette said quickly.

"Then is it because of your brother? You feel it's too soon to have a boyfriend? We've never spoken about it, but you know how sorry—"

"It's not about my brother, Didier."

They stood in awkward silence. "But you let me ask your father if I could take you out today," Didier said at last. "Your mother made us a picnic."

"Because I like you as a friend! I told my mother this morning, when she was asking about you. I said, 'Yes, I do like Didier, but not...'"

Her voice trailed away once more and Didier filled in the missing words. "As a boyfriend."

Josette nodded. "I'm sorry. But anyway, this isn't a time for boyfriends. I can only think of France."

Didier laughed loudly. "You sound like Joan of Arc."

"Are you making fun of me?" Josette said, her eyes flashing once more and her cheeks reddening.

"No," Didier said, his face instantly serious. "I know better than to make fun of you, Josette Mazet."

"Good." They stared at each other for a few moments before Josette continued. "And I'm glad I told you this, to make things clear."

"If you say so," Didier answered. "It isn't exactly what I wanted to hear." He shrugged his shoulders. "Walk back through the trees with me; there's something else in the camp you should see."

They went through the dappled shade of the overhead canopy. The camp sat on a wide, flat expanse of land, and in the distance, on all sides, were tree-covered hills.

"Take away the camp and it would be a beautiful view, wouldn't it?" Didier said.

Josette nodded.

"The hills are full of wildlife. Foxes, deer, wild boar; they all roam freely, while down there human beings are kept caged and trapped." He pointed with one extended arm. "You see that small building, near the fence closest to the road? That's the jail."

"What do you mean? They're all prisoners; the whole place is a jail."

"But that hut is special," Didier said. "If a prisoner breaks the rules or does something to upset the guards, he's locked in there for punishment. Solitary confinement. And I don't see any windows, do you? Can you imagine what it must be like on a hot summer's day like today?"

Josette fixed her gaze on the small, windowless building. "Who are the guards?"

"Gendarmes," Didier said. "And a couple of newly commissioned army officers are actually in charge of the place. I hear they've started locking up French Jews as well now. I don't know how they fit them all in."

"How did you hear?" Josette asked, turning to Didier. "How do you know all this?"

"I make it my business to know," he said softly. "That way I can stay out of trouble."

Josette stared hard at Didier, trying to read his thoughts. "Is there something you're not telling me?"

Didier laughed. "You know everything now. Oh, but there is one more thing. I'm not giving up on you, Josette.

Just because you don't want me as a boyfriend at the moment, it doesn't mean you'll feel the same in the future."

"Didier…"

"Shall we have our picnic? I'm hungry."

Josette smiled. "Yes, we'll have our…" She stopped and turned back to look at the camp. "But not here; it wouldn't be right. Let's go somewhere else."

TEN

Paul and Albert were ahead of schedule when they tied up the *Marina* at the agreed rendezvous point. After that, all they could do was be ready for a swift changeover when the new contact arrived.

Albert would reveal nothing about him beforehand. "Just in case something unfortunate has happened and our plan has been uncovered," he said. "Remember, you can't tell someone what you don't know."

Paul's small case was packed but kept hidden in the secret locker as they waited.

"Just in case," Albert had said again.

Baron, too, seemed to know that Paul was about to leave. When Paul went to stroke him behind the ear, the cat jumped up from his chair, slunk around the back of the pot-bellied stove and remained there.

"He does that when it's very cold," Albert said. "Or when he's unhappy."

The minutes ticked by, and the tension grew as the

rendezvous hour passed. Finally they heard a vehicle approach and stop at the canal side.

Albert pulled back the curtain and peered through the window. "He's here; I was starting to worry. We must move fast now, Paul." He fetched the case from its hiding place, looked at Paul for a long moment and then wrapped his arms around him. "Good luck, my young friend," he said, his voice breaking slightly. "I'll be thinking of you."

"Thank you for everything, Albert," Paul replied. He took the case and glanced towards the stove. "Are you going to say goodbye, Baron?"

Baron didn't stir.

"Come and say farewell to Paul, Baron," Albert called gently. "It may be a long time until we meet again."

There was still no movement, but then Baron's large head appeared from behind the stove, his eyes fixed on Paul. Slowly his great body emerged and he padded noiselessly across the floorboards and rubbed himself against Paul's trouser leg.

Paul reached down and stroked the cat behind his ears, setting off the loud and familiar purring. "Goodbye, Baron. Look after yourself, and Albert too."

"Come, we must go," Albert said.

He led the way up the steps and Paul followed, out onto the deck and swiftly off the *Marina* onto the canal side. Paul was caught by surprise at his first sight of the man leaning against a small black Renault.

He was younger than Albert, probably in his early forties, of average height and build, with steel-grey hair swept back from his craggy face. Most unexpectedly, he was dressed in priest's robes. He gave a smiling nod of acknowledgment as Albert and Paul approached, and held out his hand to the *Marina*'s skipper.

"It's good to see you again, my old friend. How was your journey?"

"Eventful," Albert said as they shook hands. "Paul will tell you about it later, no doubt." He turned to Paul. "This is Father Lagarde; he will keep you safe. Just don't let him bore you to death with his stories of racing cars. And certainly don't believe any of them!"

The priest turned his smiling face and striking blue eyes to Paul. "I'm very happy to meet you, Paul, but we must leave immediately. There are German patrols on the roads. I had to take a longer route than planned. That's why I am a little late."

"Go, then," Albert said, urging Paul towards the car. "We can't stand around here in the open."

"Goodbye, Albert," Paul said quickly, before climbing inside the Renault. Father Lagarde started up the car, and Paul gave a smile and a nod to Albert, who nodded in return, raising his hand in a final farewell. As the car moved slowly away from the canal side, Paul didn't look back.

For the next twenty minutes they drove in silence, Father Lagarde sensing that his passenger needed time to gather his thoughts. The Renault chugged sedately along through quiet villages, deep in the Belgian countryside, close to the border with Germany. Paul smiled as he remembered what Albert had said about Father Lagarde's stories of racing cars. At that moment, the priest appeared content to drive little faster than the *Marina* had moved at top speed.

"Did you really drive racing cars?" Paul asked eventually.

"Not just drove them, I raced them."

Father Lagarde glimpsed his look of doubt. "Paul," he said, very seriously. "I'm a priest; I don't tell lies."

Paul laughed. He was taking another step into the unknown with another stranger, but the priest was obviously doing his best to make him feel at ease, just as Albert had.

"Where are we going?" Paul asked.

Father Lagarde was French Belgian, from the south of the country, but until then, like Albert, he had spoken in Flemish, the language of the north.

"I think it would be best if we spoke in French from now on, Paul," he said, speaking in his own first language. "It will help get you used to thinking in French all the time."

"Of course," Paul answered in French.

"We're going to the town where I live," Father Lagarde continued. "It's little more than a large village really. And as it's Sunday, the busiest day of my week, I have to say mass this evening. Normally, I would be encouraging you to join us, but I think it's wisest if you stay hidden until later."

"And then what?" Paul asked.

Father Lagarde was silent for a few moments, then changed the subject. "The Bugatti Type 35," he said, "was the greatest racing car ever built. You've heard of it, of course?"

Paul shook his head. "I don't know much about motor cars."

"That's a pity," the priest replied. "Everyone should know about cars; they are the future of transport, you mark my words. One day, we'll all own a car; every family. And there will be roads built specially for them, criss-crossing every country. One day you will own a car, Paul. What do you think of that?"

Paul shrugged his shoulders. "I've never really thought about it. I did have a two-stroke motorcycle when I was in Antwerp."

Father Lagarde sighed, trying not to look too disappointed. "It's a start, I suppose."

They drove slowly through another village, passing a few elderly men sitting on a bench. They waved as the Renault went by and Father Lagarde waved back.

"Do you know them?" Paul asked.

"No, but as there aren't many cars out here in the countryside, it's a novelty for people when they see one go by. That's also why I'm driving so slowly. At this speed, if we meet a German patrol, they'll see I'm a priest and probably just wave me on my way. That's what usually happens. If I was driving faster it might be different."

The road curved sharply to the right before it left the village and Father Lagarde dropped a gear before starting the turn.

"Blast!" the priest hissed as the Renault rounded the bend.

Fifty metres ahead, a German infantryman was standing with his back to them in the middle of the road.

Father Lagarde began to slow the vehicle, but the soldier had already heard the engine. As the car approached, he turned around and raised his right arm, with the flat of his hand opened towards them a clear order to stop.

"Doesn't look as though this one's going to wave you on," Paul breathed.

"I must do as he signals," Father Lagarde said. "Do you see the motorbike by the side of the road? If I turn and drive off he'll catch me in seconds. We'll have to bluff it out."

The Renault came to a standstill a few metres from the soldier.

Father Lagarde switched off the engine and they waited for the soldier to approach. But he didn't. He stood perfectly still, studying both occupants of the vehicle closely, one hand on the shoulder strap of his rifle.

As he caught the man's eye, Paul calmly smiled and nodded, and after a moment's hesitation, the soldier smiled and nodded in return before turning his back on them.

"Of course," Father Lagarde said quietly. "It's a crossroads. He's not here to check vehicles, just to stop them. Wind down your window a little."

Paul did as instructed and after no more than a minute they heard the sound of heavy traffic approaching. Almost instantly a long convoy of German vehicles, heading north-wards, crossed in front of them. Lorries, some packed with troops, others with supplies, armoured vehicles, tank carri-ers, trucks pulling field guns; the procession took several minutes to go by.

When the last vehicle had finally passed and the cloud of dust had cleared, the soldier turned back and indicated to Father Lagarde that he could drive on. The priest needed no second invitation. He started up the Renault and pulled away, giving the soldier a nod and a wave.

They cleared the village and moved onto a long, desolate stretch of narrow road. With nothing more than the occa-sional tree on either side, Father Lagarde obviously felt it was safe to increase their speed, so he put his foot down on the accelerator. The road was bumpy and uneven but he drove confidently, and was clearly in complete control.

"You stayed very calm, Paul," he said. "I'm impressed."

Paul didn't respond, but thought back to the encounter with the German soldier. He had been tense, he realized, but not scared; anxious, but ready for whatever followed. A few days earlier it might have been different, but not now. So much had changed, including Paul himself.

He turned to Father Lagarde. "Does that mean you trust me enough to tell me what happens tonight?"

The priest considered for a moment and then smiled. "Yes, Paul, it does. Tonight, I'm driving you into France."

ELEVEN

It was nearing midnight and the silent streets of the small Belgian town where Father Lagarde lived were brilliantly illuminated under a canopy of stars.

Father Lagarde looked up and spoke in little more than a whisper. "Not perfect for travelling unobserved, but useful if I have to drive without lights."

Paul stared. "You've done that?"

The priest smiled. "Several times when I was a young man; sadly I could never resist a dare. But it's dangerous and I wouldn't choose to do it now, or advise anyone else to. Come, we must go quickly."

Suitcase in hand, Paul started towards the Renault.

"No, Paul," Father Lagarde said softly, "I'm taking you to meet an old friend."

"But you said we must go quickly."

"Exactly. Follow me."

They walked swiftly through the empty streets, the windows of every house shuttered or darkened by heavy curtains.

The town had no permanent German army presence, but Father Lagarde had explained that they were stationed nearby and frequently patrolled the area – day and night. If they met a German patrol, Father Lagarde could explain that he had been summoned to see a sick parishioner or even to administer the last rights to someone close to death. Paul had no such protection; until he reached France, when he could use his forged French papers and travel permit, he didn't even have an identity.

Moving quickly, and keeping to the shadows, they headed for the outskirts of town. Suddenly, nearby, a dog began to bark.

"Shut up, will you!" a man's voice yelled. The dog barked even louder. In the still of the night it was impossible to know for certain where the sound was coming from, but it was very close.

A light came on in the first floor of a house across the street, a dull yellow shaft spilling out into the night. Father Lagarde put out an arm to stop Paul and they both backed silently into the darkness of a doorway. The upstairs window was slightly ajar.

"I said, shut up!" the man yelled again as the dog continued to howl. "All right, I'm coming. Stupid animal!"

"I don't know why we put up with him," a woman shouted. "He never stops barking."

"He's a guard dog, isn't he!" the man came back. "Keeping us safe in our beds!"

As suddenly as it had started, the barking stopped and the night was silent again.

"Move, Paul," the priest whispered and, avoiding the light from the window, they crept away, reaching the edge of the town within minutes.

"Where does this friend of yours live?" Paul asked after they had passed the last house.

"Not far now," Father Lagarde said. "Just down that track over there."

They crossed the road, started down a mud track and walked for another fifty metres. Then, straight ahead, Paul saw the outline of a small building. It turned out to be a stone-built barn.

"Someone's in there?" Paul whispered. "Is he hiding?"

Father Lagarde didn't answer but pulled out a torch and a key from his pocket.

At the front of the building were double wooden doors, their brown paint faded and peeling. Father Lagarde slotted the key into the lock and after two turns it clicked open. The priest pulled back one of the doors, telling Paul to open the other.

The interior was shrouded in darkness until Father Lagarde flicked on his torch.

There, sitting in silent grandeur, was a beautiful horizon-blue, open-top car.

Father Lagarde's face beamed. "The Bugatti Type 35," he said proudly. "*My* Bugatti Type 35."

"This!" Paul gasped. "We're going to France in this?"

* * *

"I bought her in 1926." Father Lagarde spoke with pride, as they prepared to leave. "Raced her for the first time at Lyons later that year."

"Did you win?" Paul asked.

"Modesty forbids me to answer that," the priest replied. Then he winked and nodded. "Let's just say that in this car, I believe I can outrun any vehicle on the road. Now, be ready to crank the starting handle when I signal, and once she starts, jump in next to me."

He climbed into the driver's seat, switched on the ignition and gave Paul a thumbs-up sign.

Paul grasped the starting handle in both hands, felt the resistance point and swung the cold metal through a single turn to the right. The engine gave a slight cough, then burst into life, its throaty roar loud in the confined space of the barn.

As Paul clambered in, Father Lagarde feathered the throttle and then slipped the Bugatti into gear, and eased her gently through the barn doors.

"Shouldn't I close the doors?" Paul asked.

The priest shook his head. "I must be back here before first light. They can stay open until my return."

There was little room in the cockpit; two individual leather seats shared a single backrest. Paul was squeezed into the passenger seat with his suitcase on his lap.

As the Bugatti bumped slowly down the mud track, Paul's eyes were drawn to the control panel. It was sparse and basic; pressure and oil gauges and the rev counter were set in a simple, steel housing, from which the wooden-rimmed steering-wheel also sprouted.

Above that, on the exterior bodywork, was a small windscreen, but as they reached the turn for the road, Father Lagarde slipped a pair of goggles over his eyes and passed a second pair to Paul.

"They make it easier for us to see at speed," he said with a grin. "The lights help too." He switched on the headlights and their beams cut through the darkness. "Here we go, Paul. Next stop, France."

TWELVE

The plan was simple: drive like the wind to the agreed rendezvous point, stopping for nothing or no one.

There was no back-up plan in case of an emergency, no contingency measures; the unorthodox priest obviously didn't work that way. With Father Lagarde it was all or nothing.

He drove the Bugatti as though he were part of it, effortlessly demonstrating the difference between someone who drives a car quickly and a genuine racing driver. His entire body worked in harmony with the machine, and the Bugatti, freed from too long behind the garage doors, responded smoothly to every turn of the wheel, every change of gear, every touch of the brakes.

Father Lagarde had told Paul the engine needed to warm thoroughly before the carburettors would respond fully and he could really "open her up", as he put it. But in the first seconds, as the vehicle accelerated at the first thrust of power, Paul felt the surge of adrenaline through his body. It was thrilling, exhilarating, as if he too was free again after being imprisoned. The cold night air bit into his cheeks and made his eyes water, but he felt alive and bursting with energy as they hurtled through the darkness, the headlights barely two pinpricks of light illuminating the way ahead.

The route Father Lagarde had worked out wasn't the quickest way to their destination, but it was the safest. Driving through towns and villages where enemy soldiers were stationed was too great a risk, even for the daring priest. So they stuck to quiet back roads, not glimpsing another living soul as they zigzagged down through Belgium towards the French border.

The priest had calculated that if all went to plan there would be time to make the rendezvous point, refill the Bugatti's fuel tank and be back home before dawn. It would be tight, but he was confident he could do it.

On long stretches of flat, open road, he floored the accelerator, making the Bugatti dart forward like a thoroughbred racehorse entering the finishing straight. And as they wound their way through twists and turns in thickly wooded areas, he expertly used gears and brakes to ease the vehicle on its way.

Paul sat back and watched in admiration, speaking only when Father Lagarde spoke to him. He didn't wish to disturb the priest's concentration and was content simply to observe a master going about his business.

"There were a number of good machines around in my racing days, you know, Paul!" Father Lagarde shouted as he changed down a gear, leaned into a corner and accelerated out. "Maserati, Alfa Romeo, Delage, all excellent racing cars, but nothing quite like the Bugatti Type 35. Not for me, anyway."

"I can believe that!" Paul yelled back. "I've never been driven like this, it's incredible!"

Father Lagarde laughed. "We're very close to France now. And fortunately our German friends don't have checkpoints on the smaller roads and border crossings. There are just too many of them."

They were travelling through a densely wooded area. Racing over a small crossroads, Paul thought he caught a fleeting glimpse of a dark shape on the turning to their left.

Father Lagarde was one step ahead of him. "I think I've spoken a little too soon."

Paul looked back and immediately saw bright headlights turning towards them.

To Paul's surprise, the priest slowed the Bugatti. "I want to hear its engine," he said before Paul could speak, "to know exactly what we have on our tail."

"But…"

Father Lagarde lifted one hand from the wheel to silence him and turned his head slightly towards the other vehicle.

Hearing the high-pitched scream of its engine, Paul glanced behind and saw that the car was swiftly making up the distance between them. He flashed a look at Father Lagarde, who seemed completely unconcerned. Paul couldn't decide whether he was ice-cool or crazy.

"Ah, yes," the priest said at last, "it's a Citroën 11CV. The Germans have even taken our cars to use for themselves. It's good, but it will never get near us."

Paul looked back again. The twin headlights of the chasing vehicle shone directly into his eyes. "Actually," he said urgently, "it is getting near us, very near."

The priest nodded, dropped a gear and floored the accelerator. In seconds they were leaving the Citroën far behind.

But now Paul could see a third headlight as a smaller vehicle swung out and overtook the Citroën. "There's something else coming!" he shouted. "Faster. I think it might be a motorbike."

Father Lagarde risked a quick look back. "A motorcycle and sidecar; makes it more interesting. Keep your head down, Paul, it's just possible that—"

Before the priest could finish his sentence, a staccato burst of gunfire cut through the night air. Paul had heard that sound before; it was a submachine-gun. As the sound echoed away, a fleeting image of his father being gunned down on the dockside flashed through his mind.

The weapon spat out again.

"The passenger's firing!" Father Lagarde shouted. "A hand-held weapon. At least it's not a heavy machine-gun fitted to the sidecar; that would be much more dangerous."

Another short burst sounded and in the same instant a round grazed the side panel close to Paul's shoulder.

"My paintwork!" Father Lagarde yelled. "Now they're making me angry!"

He began swerving the Bugatti from side to side on the narrow road and Paul was acutely aware that the vehicle's fuel tank was directly behind them, beneath the thin casing of the rear bodywork. A piercing round from the submachine-gun could explode the Bugatti in a ball of flames.

But before the sidecar passenger could fire off another burst, the road curved away into a bend. The Bugatti swept majestically into the turn, engine roaring, and they were suddenly, for a few seconds at least, out of their pursuer's sight.

"I didn't really want to do this, but it will probably help," Father Lagarde said, reaching to flick off the headlights, instantly plunging them into total darkness. "Don't worry, Paul," he added, "we'll soon get our night vision."

Within seconds, and with the aid of starlight, Paul could see the road ahead. He couldn't see very far, and neither could Father Lagarde, but the priest's incredible reflexes and uncanny instinct kept the Bugatti in the centre of the road at high speed.

Paul looked back as the motorcycle and sidecar emerged from the bend. He couldn't help imagining the German soldiers' confusion as they realized the road ahead was empty and the car they were chasing had vanished into the night.

The bike slowed briefly, its rider and passenger checking to see if the Bugatti had spun off the road. But then its speed increased again.

Paul saw yellow flashes as another shot burst out from the submachine-gun.

"Just trying his luck!" Father Lagarde yelled. "He can't see us. Or maybe he's shooting at pigeons."

They sped on for another two kilometres, increasing the distance between the Bugatti and its pursuers. Then, up ahead, the road forked.

"I know this place," the priest said. "And if I'm right, the Germans will expect us to take the right fork."

He turned left, drove on for another two hundred metres and pulled the Bugatti to the side of the road. They looked back, and waited.

Seconds ticked by and then they saw the single headlight beam and heard the engine as the bike approached the fork. It slowed, almost to a standstill.

"Making his mind up," Father Lagarde said quietly.

The motorbike's engine roared and the beam turned to the right and went flickering away. A minute later, the Citroën's headlights appeared again and swiftly disappeared in the same direction.

Father Lagarde slipped the Bugatti into gear and drove on.

Ten minutes later, he turned to his passenger and smiled. "That didn't go quite the way I planned, but welcome to France."

About a hundred metres ahead and to their left, three faint pinpricks of light blinked in the darkness.

"Look," Paul said.

"Yes, I saw it," the priest answered. He drove slowly onwards. After a few seconds the flashes came again.

"That's them," Father Lagarde said.

Half an hour ago they had entered French territory and Paul felt that it was at last safe for him to ask a question. "Where are we?"

"In champagne country," the priest replied. "To the south-east of the city of Reims."

He turned the Bugatti off the road at the entrance to a farm and continued slowly down a smooth mud track into a square yard with open barns on two sides and a house on another.

A figure standing in the darkness of the closest barn flicked the torchlight over the ground and the Bugatti followed it until the light stopped moving. Father Lagarde switched off the engine. The night was totally silent.

The priest turned to Paul and lifted the goggles from his face. He looked like a weary owl, dust and grime surrounding large white circles where the goggles had been. But within the circles, his blue eyes still sparkled. "We made it, Paul."

Paul nodded. "Thank you," he said, removing his own pair.

Footsteps sounded and Paul glanced across to see what appeared to be a short man wearing farm overalls and a cap approaching. It was only when the figure stopped at the driver's side that Paul realized his mistake. There, bathed in yellow torchlight, stood a young woman of around twenty. She was small and slim, and the chestnut hair beneath the cap framed delicate features.

"I'm Sabine Simorre," she said to Father Lagarde. "My parents are in the house. They have a meal and hot coffee ready for you."

"Thank you," the priest answered, "both will be most welcome. I'm Father Lagarde and this is my young friend, Paul."

Paul nodded weakly, certain that he looked as stupid as he felt. He didn't know many women, especially attractive young woman like Sabine Simorre.

She in turn was studying his face intently. "Mmmm," she said, apparently disappointed. Before Paul could think of what to say she added, "You look a bit English."

Paul glanced at Father Lagarde for guidance, and when none came said simply, "That's because I am a bit English."

THIRTEEN

Josette was confused. And when Josette was confused she was unhappy. She was of strong and uncomplicated opinion; what was right was right and what was wrong was wrong. It was as simple as that.

To Josette the problem for her beloved France, and its solution, were both blatantly obvious. The problem was the Nazis and the Vichy government; the solution was to get rid of them. She knew that wouldn't be easy, but it was the only answer. Why, wondered Josette, didn't everyone else feel the same way?

People she had known and liked for most of her life had suddenly changed. Proud Frenchmen and women didn't seem to care that their country had been ripped in two. Or if they did, they weren't prepared to do anything about it. Worse still, some were collaborating with the new government for their own ends, betraying former friends and neighbours.

And it wasn't just in Lavelanet and the surrounding area.

Stories of betrayal were circulating throughout southern France. It was confusing, frustrating, disappointing – and Josette didn't understand it at all. Which was why she had come to see her grandmother, Odile Mazet, her father's mother.

The two had always been close. They shared similar looks and the same fiery temperament. Odile was seventy now and had mellowed a little, but she retained a razor-sharp mind, and was always prepared to voice her opinions and defend her point of view, however controversial it might be. Just like her granddaughter.

Odile lived across the town from the Mazet family house in an old, end-of-terrace, stone-built cottage nestling close to the river Touyre.

Josette had come there straight after work and now they were sitting in the little lean-to attached to the back of the house. They had spoken about the family, about Josette's continuing worries for her mother's depression and about the increasing prices at Lavelanet's Friday market. Odile knew that there was something else on her granddaughter's mind, but she enjoyed Josette's company so was content to wait until she was ready to mention it.

"Gra-mere," Josette said at last, using, as she always had, the less formal version of "grandmother", "why is it that so many people don't seem to care about what's happening to France, or won't do anything about it?"

Odile sat back in her wicker chair and glanced through

the window to the swiftly flowing river, weighing her thoughts before replying. "It's little more than twenty years since the last war; the war they said would end all wars. A lot of us lost loved ones then; for me it was a cousin and a nephew, for others it was husbands and sons. For some – " she looked across at Josette " – a brother or a grandson."

She paused and Josette knew they were both thinking about Venant.

"Many French people have had enough of war," Odile continued. "They can't face any more, so they put it to the back of their minds, ignore it completely. That way, it's almost as though it isn't happening."

"But it *is* happening," Josette said, her anger rising. "And it won't go away unless we all try to do something about it. But Papa says I mustn't get involved, and Didier Brunet thinks the same…"

"Ah, Didier," Odile said, "I know his family. His father was wounded in the last war and he never really got over what he'd been through. He died when young Didier was about five, I think. Did you know that?"

Josette shook her head. "What happened?"

"An accident," Odile said sadly, "in the mountains. He fell, although some say…' Her voice trailed off for a moment. "I think he couldn't live any longer with what he'd seen. Perhaps that's why Didier doesn't want to get involved. And as for your mother and father—"

"What?" Josette said. "What about them?"

"Your father fought in the last war too."

"He never speaks about it."

Odile sighed. "What is there to say now? It's over, the people we loved have gone, and we haven't learned the lessons. Try to imagine what it's been like for your mother, Josette. In the last war she waited for the man she loved to come home, dreading every day that a letter would arrive telling her he'd been killed. Instead they married and had a son. And then twenty years later that son is killed, within days of a new war starting."

She looked towards the window again and Josette found herself thinking that, for the first time, her grandmother looked old and tired. She considered her words carefully before replying. "Yes, I suppose ... I suppose I can understand. But what about those who are actually siding with the Nazis, the collaborators?"

"I can't answer for them," her grandmother said with a shrug of her shoulders. "Not everyone has the principles that you do."

"It's awful that people can't trust each other any more," Josette said, growing angry again. "You see it, everywhere. In the factory, people I've known all my life are like strangers, whispering in corners. It's suddenly all so ..." she paused, searching for the right words "... uncomfortable and ... unsettling."

"I see it too," Odile said. "People are afraid."

"Even old friends," Josette said. "People you always

thought you could rely on. You know the gendarme officer, Gaston Rouzard, Papa's friend. He's been here for ever. I'm sure he's a collaborator."

"And what makes you say that?"

"I've seen him. Spying, listening. I know he was listening when Jean-Pierre Dilhat was speaking at the café."

"Speaking about what?"

"Taking action, but being careful, secretive. Using code-names instead of real names, that sort of thing."

"Dangerous talk."

"I know, but when when Gaston left I followed him…"

"Josette!"

"He didn't see me, but I watched him writing in a note-book. He must have been noting down everything Jean-Pierre said."

"Josette, you must not go around making accusations."

"I haven't told anyone; no one but you."

A sudden burst of rainfall thumped on the conservatory roof like machine-gun fire, making them both look upwards.

"I worry about you, Josette," Odile said. "You have such a quick temper."

"Like you?"

"Yes, like me, but that's not good. Sometimes I wish you were a little more like your father. Calmer."

Henri Mazet stood on the factory floor, watching the rain-drops pound down onto the building's huge glass skylights.

Summer was over, although even during the height of the season, the closeness of Lavelanet to the Pyrenees meant that a sudden downpour or even a violent storm was always possible. September and October usually brought further days of glorious sunshine, with azure skies and fierce heat. Soon though, the autumn nights would turn bitterly cold, however strongly the sun blazed during the day.

As Henri watched the rain he gently smoothed down the bristles of his moustache with his right index finger. He had a lot on his mind. Production in the factory had to be kept up; his wife, Hélène, showed no signs of emerging from the depression that had struck her since the loss of their son; and his daughter, Josette – she appeared to want to take on the entire German army and win the war single-handedly.

Henri sighed at the thought of war. It was as though there had been no true peace in Europe since the end of the First World War. Nations had steadily built up their arsenals; politicians and generals had bullied and threatened and invaded their neighbours; just over the mountains in Spain the vicious civil war had only recently ended. And now France was in turmoil again, the country and its people divided. Henri wanted only peace, a real and permanent peace this time. But he knew his responsibilities; he would do his duty, however unpopular that might prove to be.

Henri was alone in the factory. The machines were still and silent, the main doors locked. He glanced again at the rain, then walked back towards his office. He hoped some better weather would last into autumn, as it usually did. It was important for many reasons, not least because sunshine generally put a smile on the faces on the factory floor.

As Henri walked along the aisles of machines, he heard the bell ring at the entrance door. He checked his watch; his visitor was exactly on time.

Josette clutched the umbrella her grandmother had insisted she take and hurried through the rain, thinking about their conversation, and especially about her father and Didier.

She understood now their reluctance to become involved in the fight for freedom – but that didn't mean she wouldn't try to change their minds.

Her eyes hardened as she thought about the collaborators who lurked in and around Lavelanet, people like the gendarme officer, Gaston Rouzard. There could be no understanding and no forgiveness for people like him. As far as Josette was concerned, they should be rounded up and made to face the firing squad. They were the scum of the earth and deserved no mercy. That was the way it had always been with traitors. And the way it should be now.

Josette had to pass the factory on her way home. Approaching, she saw the light burning in her father's first-floor office. He must be working late. Again.

The rain showed no sign of relenting, so she hurried across the street, deciding to collect her father so they could walk home together. She was going to be better with him, she told herself; less judgemental, more understanding, more tolerant. Papa deserved that.

The front door was unlocked. "Typical." Josette sighed to herself. Burglars could empty the safe of the weekly wage packets and Papa wouldn't notice.

She left the soaking umbrella on the entrance mat and climbed the stairs. The steady rain pounding on the roof drowned the sound of her footsteps as she walked along the corridor. But just before she reached the corner by the office she stopped. She could hear men's voices, her father's and another she did not recognize. She couldn't make out what they were saying.

She pressed herself against the wall.

The office was half-windowed. Josette knew that if she peered around the corner she would see whoever was inside the room. Slowly, she edged forward, feeling guilty for spying on her father but certain that all was not right. Inch by inch, she craned her neck closer to the corner. And then she saw.

They were sitting facing each other – her father and Gaston Rouzard.

Josette drew back, her mind racing. Her father, meeting in secret with Gaston. What did it mean? What *could* it mean?

And then, as she heard Rouzard's voice, she got her answer – the answer she dreaded. "And as for Jean-Pierre

Dilhat; we must do something about him, Henri. We must."

Josette felt dizzy, stunned. For a moment she felt as though her legs would give way and she might faint. She leaned against the wall, breathing deeply and hardly able to see. The voices were blurred now, like her muddled thoughts and cloudy vision.

She clenched both hands into fists, forcing her fingernails into the flesh of her palms until they hurt so much that all she could think of was the pain. The dizziness had gone. She wasn't going to faint; she wouldn't allow herself to faint. Not for a couple of traitors, even if one of them was her father.

Silently, she hurried away.

FOURTEEN

"Your name is?"

"Philippe Héroux."

"And your age?"

"Seventeen."

"Your date of birth?"

"The seventh of May, nineteen twenty-three."

"And why are you travelling?"

"My cousin and I are going to see our grandmother, she's very ill."

"I see. And where does your grandmother live?"

"In Dole."

Sabine nodded. "That was very good, especially getting the date of birth right without hesitating. Well done, Paul."

"Thanks."

"*No!*" Sabine thumped the arm of her chair in frustration. "How many times must I say it? You're Philippe, not Paul! Paul doesn't exist while you're with me!"

"I'm sorry, I thought—"

"No, you didn't. You *didn't* think! And you must be thinking all the time. That's the oldest trick in the book, and you fell for it."

"But if I'm questioned, they won't know my real name."

Sabine leaned forward in her chair. "How do you know what they know? You have no idea what they know and neither do I. That's why you must be Philippe Héroux at every moment. Your papers say you're Philippe Héroux and you have a travel permit in the name of Philippe Héroux. That's who you are. And if you want to survive, you'd better believe it."

"All right, I'm sorry," Paul snapped irritably, angry with himself rather than anything Sabine had said. She was right; he'd made a stupid mistake. They had practised the cover story endlessly and Paul thought he was completely ready for the journey they were about to make.

"I won't get it wrong again."

"I hope not," Sabine said, getting up, "for both our sakes."

She was dressed very differently from the night when they had first met. She wore a dark grey pleated skirt and a woollen jumper in a lighter shade of grey. She had plain black shoes on and now, as Paul watched, she slid into a grey gabardine raincoat, which she belted tightly. Finally she pushed most of her hair under a black beret, and then checked her appearance in a wall mirror.

"Suitably plain and grey," she told her reflection. "Certainly not someone who would stand out in a crowd."

"I wouldn't say that," Paul said, instantly feeling his cheeks redden.

Reflected in the mirror, he saw Sabine raise her eyebrows and look at him. "Well, I would. I don't want to be noticed." She smiled. "It's going to be difficult enough to make the Germans or the French police believe the tall, handsome, fair-haired young man – who looks more English than French – is actually my cousin. I don't want to give them any help."

Paul blushed even more. "Do I really look more English than French?"

"Are you kidding?" she said with a laugh. "You look more English than ... than the Tower of London."

"It's from my father. His father was English, and I think before that—"

"Philippe!"

Paul stopped mid-sentence. Sabine's reflected eyes were boring into his.

"Who are you?" she demanded.

"I'm Philippe Héroux. And I'm travelling with my cousin to see our grandmother in Dole. She's very ill."

Sabine sighed and turned to face Paul, her dark brown eyes softening. "All right, just for a moment I'll speak to you as Paul, but after this it's Philippe, and only Philippe. Understood?"

Paul nodded and Sabine returned to her chair. "I don't know the details and I don't want to," she said, "but I do know that something terrible must have happened to you in Belgium and that now you're in terrible danger. That's why you're here and that's why everyone is working so hard to get you to freedom. Am I correct?"

Paul nodded again but said nothing.

"Whatever happened, I can see that it's hurting you deeply. It was obvious from the moment you arrived. I'm very sorry for you, and I realize you can't forget what happened, that's impossible, but from now you must force it to the back of your mind. You must be Philippe and not Paul; you must think and act as Philippe. Because it's not just your life that's at stake, it's mine and the other members of my group. I'm going to do everything I can for you, Paul, but you must play your part too; you must take some responsibility. Can you do that?"

"Yes, I can," Paul answered instantly. "I won't let you down, I promise."

Sabine stood up. She smiled and patted him on the shoulder. "Then get your case and jacket and we'll be on our way – *Philippe*."

Paul's stay at the isolated farm had been brief. On the first night, Father Lagarde had departed after a quick meal. Paul was shown to a bedroom. It was his first time in a proper bed for several days and he sank wearily into the soft feather mattress and instantly into a deep sleep.

He woke nine hours later to learn from Sabine that Father

Lagarde had radioed a message confirming his safe arrival back home, with no further mishaps on the return journey.

Paul was relieved by the news. As he devoured fried eggs and cured ham he thought about the way both Father Lagarde and Albert had risked everything to ferry him across Belgium and down into France. They had ignored the danger to themselves, done their job and then returned to their everyday lives. There had been scares, but luck had been on their side. And Paul knew that neither barge captain nor priest would hesitate to help the next escapee. And the next. And the one after that. They would help for as long as the war lasted or their luck held.

Paul finished his meal, sat back in his chair and took in his new surroundings. His eyes came to rest on a framed photograph of Sabine and her parents. He instantly thought of his own parents, and the dreadful fear over the fate of his mother returned. Where was she? Locked in some dank, airless prison cell? Suffering at the hands of Nazi torturers? Was she even alive? The thoughts were unbearable. Paul prayed that word would come through that she had been released and was safe. But with each passing day his doubts and his fears increased.

And a new horror had entered his mind. The picture of his father lying dead on the ground was already imprinted on his brain, and a second, almost unbearable image had joined it. Paul saw his father's lifeless body being dragged away, flung into the back of a lorry and then thrown into an unmarked grave on the outskirts of the city. Each time the nightmare came, he woke in a cold sweat. And as he lay in the darkness waiting for sleep to return, he told himself that one day he would return to Antwerp to find his father's body and give him a proper burial.

But there was little time to dwell on dark thoughts as the remainder of Paul's day was spent working with Sabine on his new identity and their cover story. He didn't even know if Sabine Simorre was the real name of the young woman who patiently, but relentlessly, went over and over each detail. Many agents had started using codenames as an added precaution, she said. Paul didn't press for more information.

In the evening, Sabine's parents returned from the fields and shared a dinner of steamed chicken and potatoes, which was eaten mainly in silence. Paul was not told the name of Sabine's parents; he was quickly learning the "need to know" rules. He asked no questions about the farm. He didn't know if animals grazed in the pastures, or if crops had recently been harvested in the fields, or if champagne grapes, almost ready for picking, still clung to the vines. He didn't need to know so he didn't ask.

With the meal over and little to talk about, Paul turned in early. But this time sleep didn't come easily. The feather mattress seemed too soft, and when he finally drifted off, it was into a troubled sleep. Then the nightmare returned.

* * *

But now Paul was about to set out on the next leg of his flight to safety. He slipped his jacket on and caught his reflection in the mirror. This time he would be travelling openly, in full view of any potential enemy. From now on, he was Philippe Héroux, and he had to play his part perfectly.

He picked up his case and followed Sabine out into the yard, where her father waited behind the wheel of an ancient, open-backed farm truck.

Paul guessed the vehicle was as old, if not older, than Father Lagarde's Bugatti, but, unlike the racing car, it was more or less a wreck. The bodywork was rusted, the thin tyres virtually tread-less and the wooden side panels were rotted and cracked.

Twenty or more hessian sacks, all tied at the neck with thick string, were stacked on the back. Sabine saw Paul glance at them as they clambered up into the cab. "We have to be taking something somewhere in case we're stopped," she said by way of explanation.

They travelled with the windows wound down. The cab was cramped and hot, and smelled of oil and the farmyard. Paul gazed out at the unfamiliar countryside, taking little in, reminding himself constantly that his name was Philippe Héroux, and running through Sabine's instructions in case they were questioned: answer clearly and briefly; don't be hesitant or uncertain, but don't be too helpful or say too much – as though desperate to say the right thing.

The first part of the journey was uneventful, with little

traffic on the roads, until they reached the outskirts of Reims. Sabine's father brought the truck to a standstill in a quiet side street.

"We get out here," Sabine told Paul.

She kissed her father on the cheek and Paul heard him whisper, "Come back safely."

They climbed down from the cab, and before shutting the door, Paul thanked the man whose name he would never know.

Sabine's father gave him a half-smile and a nod. "Good luck."

Belching oily smoke, the truck chugged slowly away. As soon as it had turned the corner, Sabine led Paul down a narrow passageway between two cottages, then through a gate into a minute backyard.

In one corner was a brick-built outside lavatory. Paul couldn't help grinning as he spotted the heart-shaped hole cut into the door – conveniently situated at eye level so that anyone could look inside to see if it was occupied.

Alongside the tiny building, five wire-fronted wooden hutches were stacked on top of one another. Inside each hutch a pink-eyed, long-eared rabbit chewed steadily on vegetable peelings. Continuing to chew, all five rabbits turned their heads and watched as Sabine and Paul stepped into the yard.

Resting against the fence next to the cages were two black bicycles, one with a wicker basket on the front and the other with a small metal rack mounted above the rear wheel.

"You can ride a bicycle?" Sabine asked.

"Of course."

"Fix your case to the one with the rack, and I'll put my bag in the basket on the other."

Less than a minute later they were cycling away, Sabine in front. She obviously knew Reims well; she rode without stopping or even pausing to check directions as they headed through the historic streets towards the main railway station.

Approaching the city centre they were waved unchallenged through a checkpoint and emerged into a wide, tree-lined boulevard, busy with pedestrians and vehicles. German soldiers were everywhere. Officers strolled leisurely in the early autumn sunshine while infantrymen stood on guard outside strategically important buildings, or marched in small squads to some other destination.

Soldiers, and the occasional passing military vehicle, were the only signs of the present war, but as Paul and Sabine cycled down the Rue des Romains, they glimpsed reminders of an earlier conflict. Huge swathes of the city had been badly damaged by German bombing during the First World War and some buildings remained unrepaired.

As they neared the station, they glimpsed in the distance the majestic twin towers of the Notre-Dame Cathedral, traditionally where the crowning of French kings had taken place. In the early days of the First World War, German shellfire had destroyed much of the building and in the blazing inferno that followed even more was lost.

They were cycling side by side now. Sabine spoke softly, taking the opportunity to remind Paul once more of his changed identity. "Do you know, Philippe, they started restoring our shattered cathedral almost as soon as the last war finished, and it's been going on ever since. They only fully reopened the building two years ago." She shook her head sadly. "Just in time for another war."

Reaching the station, Sabine dismounted and led the way to a row of bicycle stands. "They'll be collected," she said, anticipating Paul's question.

Paul glanced towards the station's high-arched doorway and took a deep breath. He was about to discover how good a job the forger had made of his new papers. And how good he would be at being someone else.

FIFTEEN

Two armed German soldiers were inspecting passengers'
documents as they passed through the checkpoint leading to the platforms.

"Remember," Sabine breathed, "if you get through
unchallenged, go straight onto the platform. Don't hang
around looking nervous; act as though you expect me to
join you."

She had said earlier that if for any reason she was stopped
and taken away, he was to travel onwards alone. He knew
their destination and where to meet the next contact. If necessary he would have to do it on his own.

Paul joined the short queue at the checkpoint and waited
his turn. He could feel his heart thudding; he had never
stood face to face with a German soldier. He felt edgy, but
reckoned that everyone in the queue would be feeling edgy
at a moment like this. The Germans might pick on anyone
for questioning.

Paul reached the front of the queue and made eye contact

with the soldier as he handed over his identity card and travel pass.

"Don't look furtive or shifty," Sabine had told him, "and don't look as though you've got something to hide."

The soldier studied both documents. He looked at the photograph on the identity card, then at Paul, and then at the photograph again. With a final cursory glance at Paul he handed back the documents and gave a curt nod. Paul was through.

Sabine passed through the checkpoint equally quickly and they strolled down the platform until they came to a spot where they could wait for their train and speak quietly without being overheard.

"We've been lucky so far," Sabine said quietly. "Don't expect it to last. Anything can happen, remember that."

Paul nodded, reminding himself to appear calm and relaxed, and recalling Sabine's words in their final briefing. "Be inconspicuous; try to be invisible."

It wasn't easy, especially when a German officer walked up to them and stopped, catching Paul's eye. He nodded and Paul hesitantly nodded back, wondering what would come next. The officer gave a slight smile of acknowledgment, checked his watch and turned away.

Paul was relieved when the station announcer's voice informed them that the train for Dijon was approaching. Dijon was where they had to change to a branch line for Dole.

With a clanking of metal on metal and a shriek of brakes, the great black steam engine drew slowly into the station, belching thick clouds of smoke.

Casually Sabine took Paul's arm and led him a little further down the platform, away from the German officer. He was the last person they wanted to be sitting opposite all the way to Dijon.

They boarded a carriage and walked along the corridor, looking into the compartments for vacant seats. Many were almost full, but eventually they came to one containing just three passengers, a young man and two nuns.

Sabine caught Paul's arm and gestured to him to go inside. He opened the door and Sabine followed him in. Paul lifted his case onto the luggage rack and took a window seat opposite one of the nuns. She smiled and he smiled back, then he settled into his seat with Sabine beside him.

Out on the platform the final passengers were boarding. A few minutes later the engine's whistle screamed and the train drew slowly out of Reims station.

They were slowing for a station stop when the compartment's sliding door suddenly flew open, causing one of the nuns, who had been dozing peacefully, to wake with a start.

Two French police officers stood in the doorway.

"Papers, please," said the first.

The second officer remained by the door as the first moved to the window where Paul and the other nun sat.

The nun offered her papers, which the officer took.

Paul waited, reminding himself to keep his answers simple if questioned, not to say too much, be too helpful or appear anxious. He stole a glance at Sabine. She was looking at the young man sitting in the opposite corner by the door. Paul could see that he was nervous. He was staring at the floor and small beads of sweat had broken out on his forehead.

The officer turned to Paul, took his papers and ran his eyes over them. It seemed to Paul that he wasn't checking them very thoroughly.

"Why are you travelling?"

"I'm going to see my grandmother," Paul answered. "With my cousin." He put a hand on Sabine's arm.

The officer's eyes flicked onto Sabine. "Our grandmother is very ill," she told him calmly.

"Where does she live?" the officer asked, his eyes on Paul again.

"In Dole."

The nun sitting opposite Paul sighed and gave him a sympathetic smile. "We'll pray for your grandmother," she said gently.

Apparently satisfied with the answers, the officer handed back Paul's documents, took Sabine's and scanned them briefly.

He turned to the nun who had been dozing. Her papers were checked and as the train continued to slow, he moved to the young man. Paul and Sabine looked in his direction and immediately saw, outside in the corridor, the German officer who had waited next to Paul on the platform.

Paul went cold. At the same moment he felt Sabine stiffen at his side. This was it. Something had gone terribly wrong and their carefully planned subterfuge had been discovered.

"Papers."

The police officer was still looking at the young man, who reached into a pocket and produced his papers.

"Where are you travelling to?"

"Beaune," was the one-word answer.

"Why are you going to Beaune?"

The young man hesitated before slowly and very deliberately giving his reply. "I sell wine."

The few heavily accented words made it obvious that the young man was English.

The train had stopped. Paul and Sabine watched as the German officer stepped into the doorway, drew a Lugar P08 pistol from its holster and pointed it at the Englishman. "We are not satisfied with your answers," he said in clipped English. "Come with me, please."

The young man's head sank down onto his chest and he gave an anguished sigh of despair. He stood up and, for an instant, his hands moved upwards, as though to grab the pistol.

But the officer was ready. He took a small backward step

into the corridor. "Please don't attempt anything silly," he said quickly. "I'm quite prepared to fire. And even if you did get past me, there are armed soldiers all over the station. You see, we've been expecting you, Lieutenant Conway."

The questioning and arrest had been perfectly timed. The Englishman's whole body appeared to sag, knowing his bid for freedom was over. He nodded, shuffled slowly from the compartment and disappeared along the corridor, accompanied by the French policemen.

The German officer looked across the compartment at the remaining passengers, smiled and switched back to French as he said, "Sorry for any disturbance. I wish you all a pleasant onward journey."

SIXTEEN

"**I** wanted to help him," Paul said.

"Of course, you did," Sabine answered. "I did too, but there was nothing we could do without compromising our own situation. And even then, what could we do?"

Paul didn't answer, but he knew Sabine was right.

They had changed trains at Dijon for the short onward journey to Dole. The branch line train was carrying far fewer passengers and Paul and Sabine were alone in a compartment so could speak freely.

"Sadly he'll never know," Sabine continued, "but his being captured like that certainly helped us. The guards were so concerned with arresting him it didn't occur to them there could be someone else they were looking for in the very same compartment."

It was true. After the young Englishman had been marched away under heavy guard, Paul and Sabine were not troubled again.

"I suppose you're right," Paul said. "But now he'll

spend the rest of the war in a prison camp."

Sabine shrugged. "I don't know. He was on the run. He must have escaped the Germans once, maybe he'll do it again." She nodded towards the window. "We're coming into Dole."

Dole stood on the Doubs river and was close to the Demarcation Line, the newly imposed border separating Occupied France from the so-called "Free Zone".

The Germans had quickly realized that France was too big for total occupation, so they had handed the control of a vast central and southern area to the Vichy Government. Everyone knew this zone was far from free; but at least it was free from German soldiers.

"We're going to a café in the old town," Sabine said as they stepped from the carriage onto the platform. "Our contact should be waiting for us."

"Do you know him?" Paul asked.

Sabine laughed as she replied. "Yes, I know him."

"What's so funny?"

"We're related," Sabine said softly, and then almost in a whisper. "He really is my cousin."

Paul raised his eyebrows in surprise. For once, Sabine had revealed unessential information, something he didn't need to know. He said nothing but was pleased that her confidence in him had grown.

The checkpoint at the small station office was unmanned so they wandered through and out into Dole. They strode briskly through the narrow streets, past the river and the canal into the old centre, where picturesque medieval buildings huddled together like conspirators involved in a secret plot.

A stocky man in his twenties sat alone on the café terrace, nursing an empty coffee cup. He stood as he saw Sabine and Paul approach, then kissed Sabine on both cheeks and offered his hand to Paul. "Louis Bourdon."

"Philippe Héroux," Paul replied without hesitation.

"Shall we go?" Louis said, and without giving them a chance to answer, he strode away, dodging down one narrow street after another until they came to a long row of tall houses. Louis approached a front door and tapped lightly. It was opened almost immediately by an elderly, bald-headed man, with a pink face and rimless spectacles.

"Come in, come in," he said quickly, standing back so they could enter.

"This is André, he's going to take your photograph," Louis said to Paul as soon as the front door was closed.

"My photograph?"

"For your new papers."

"New? But I already—"

"You need different papers for when you're travelling in the Free Zone. The papers are ready; we only need to add your name and the photograph. You can have your real first name again this time; it will make life a lot easier. What is it?"

Paul looked at Sabine. She had told him so many times

that for as long as they were together he was Philippe; he almost feared to speak his own name.

But Sabine smiled. "It's Paul."

Paul was at Louis Bourdon's house, just a few streets away from André's place. The photograph had been taken and the new documents were to be delivered the following morning. That same evening, under cover of darkness, Louis would lead Paul over the Demarcation Line into the Free Zone.

In the meantime, all they could do was wait. And waiting was difficult for Paul. Waiting, with nothing to occupy him, brought back agonizing memories, horrifying images of his father's death, and the aching dread over the fate of his mother.

Paul had washed, changed his clothes and was sitting on the bed in his small attic bedroom when there was a soft tap on the door.

"Yes?"

The door swung open and Sabine appeared. She was staying the night, as it would be impossible to get back to the farm before the ten o'clock curfew. "Louis has made some supper," she said. "It's ready."

"You could have called me."

Sabine shook her head. "We have to be careful. Shouting or even speaking too loudly might draw attention to the house. There are neighbours Louis believes can't be trusted."

She noticed Paul sigh.

"Are you OK?"

He frowned. "It's as though no one can be trusted."

"These days it's best to think that way," Sabine said. "At least until you are absolutely certain."

"I was thinking about my mother." Paul saw the look of wariness that came into Sabine's eyes. "I know," he said quickly. "I know I'm not supposed to talk about what's happened, but that doesn't mean I can stop my thoughts. And my dreams."

Sabine paused for a moment before replying. "I … I do know a little of what happened," she said. "And from what I've learned it seems to me that you're very brave."

"No," Paul said, "I'm not. Not brave like you. Or Louis, or Father Lagarde, or Albert. All risking your lives for someone you don't even know."

"But I do know you now … Paul," Sabine said with a smile. "Come on, let's eat."

They went down the steep wooden staircase into the kitchen. A dim ceiling light burned in the centre of the room and closed shutters kept out prying eyes.

"Sit," Louis ordered. "It's ready."

The hearty rabbit stew made Paul feel better and by the time the meal was over he was ready to ask about the following evening.

"Is it difficult to cross the Demarcation Line?" he said to Louis.

"Depends," Louis answered with a shrug. "It's not

literally a barrier stretching from one side of France to the other. There *are* barriers in various places, with armed guards on duty all the time. In other places there are fences and wire. But we won't be crossing at any of these."

"Then where?"

Louis laughed. "Somewhere where there's nothing but a sign stuck in a field, or a marker post. Or nothing at all. You'll see."

"You're so close to the line here," Paul said. "Haven't you thought of crossing yourself and staying in the Free Zone?"

Louis stood up and glanced at Sabine. "Coffee?"

"Please."

"And for you?" Louis said to Paul, who shook his head.

Louis went to the stove, put water on to boil, then reached into a cupboard and brought out a tin.

"I have friends living on the other side," he said. "This 'line' has separated families, cut people off from their friends and their work, even kids from their schools. As far as I'm concerned there's little difference which side of the line you're on. The whole of France will be a prison until we free ourselves of the Germans. I prefer to do what I can from this side."

Paul nodded and they sat in silence until Louis brought the coffee back to the table.

"I have something else to tell you," Louis said as he sat down. "Not good news, I'm afraid."

Paul's heart almost stopped beating. It was news of his mother; it had to be.

"It's Jos Theys," Louis said. "We picked up a radio message from Belgium. He's been arrested; taken in for questioning by the Germans. And others in Antwerp have been taken too."

"And my mother," Paul blurted out. "Have you heard … is there any…?"

"I'm sorry, I'm afraid I know nothing about your mother."

"But they must have said something… She was taken—"

Sabine reached across and rested a hand on Paul's arm. "There's nothing more to tell, Paul," she said gently. "You know as much as we do."

Paul sat back in his chair. The uncertainty of events in Antwerp was far more terrifying than the prospect of escaping to southern France and across the mountains into Spain. But he couldn't allow himself to dwell on Antwerp; it was too painful. He looked at Louis. "What happens after we've crossed the line tomorrow night?"

"We have a long walk," Louis replied. "Then we rendezvous with a friend of mine, and he'll take us closer to Lyon railway station."

"And then?"

"And then," Louis said, his face suddenly serious, "until you meet your final contact in the south, you'll be on your own."

SEVENTEEN

This was no gentle stroll in the countryside; it was more like a forced march. And this time, without stars to help guide the way, the night was pitch black. Louis refused to use a torch, saying that even a single narrow beam might be spotted from miles away by an alert crossing guard.

They were walking side by side along a narrow lane, Louis maintaining a punishing pace. Paul had struggled at first. But just as it had when Father Lagarde switched off the Bugatti's headlights, Paul's night vision kicked in, and soon he could see well enough to walk without stumbling. And now he had his second wind, he was comfortably matching Louis stride for stride.

Few words were exchanged, giving Paul plenty of time to think about the news of Jos Theys's arrest. Jos had been right, Paul thought. There had to be a traitor in the Antwerp group. And after Jos, who would be next? Albert? Father Lagarde? Sabine? With one arrest leading to another, the Resistance movement in Belgium and northern France could collapse like a house of cards.

The night was deathly quiet. Occasionally the screech of a nocturnal bird cut through the air, or a small animal rustling in the roadside undergrowth. Otherwise only their footsteps broke the silence. Perfectly in time and as regular as a metronome, they sounded like a single person striding steadily through the darkness.

They took a left turn, heading south, and a few minutes later Louis came to a halt. "We'll rest here and eat," he said softly, nodding towards a gap in the hedge.

The night was still warm, but the rough grass in the little clearing was already damp with dew. Louis took off his jacket and sat on it, gesturing to Paul to do the same before delving into a canvas bag for the food. Paul sank to the ground, grateful for a short rest, though glad to be travelling again, he realized.

Sabine had departed early, and Louis and Paul had also left the house in daylight. In a town of twenty thousand people it was easier to go unnoticed during the day.

Following the course of the river for a mile or so outside the town, they had eventually arrived at the place Louis had decided would be their lay-up point. It was a small copse, off the track and out of sight of any passers-by.

They waited until well after nightfall before beginning the long trek that had brought them to this latest resting place.

Paul finished an apple and a hunk of cheese, thinking that

they must have covered at least eight kilometres so far. But there were many more kilometres and many hours of travelling ahead before he would finally meet with the contact who would organize his escape across the Pyrenees.

"What's the name of the contact in Lavelanet?" he asked.

"I don't know his real name," Louis replied, "and you know by now that even if I did, I wouldn't tell you. His code-name is Renard."

Paul smiled. "The fox."

"Let's hope he has the fox's cunning," Louis said. "He's heading the new Resistance movement down there."

"And how will I know Renard?"

"You won't; he'll know you. He'll be waiting when you reach Montpellier station."

Paul shivered; the temperature was dropping quickly.

Louis noticed it too. "Put your coat on," he said, getting to his feet and picking up his own jacket. "We'll soon get warm."

He was right. Paul quickly felt warmer as they strode purposefully on. Twenty minutes later Louis pointed to his left, leapt over a shallow ditch and began hiking across an open field.

Paul followed, struggling to catch up; the going was harder, as the field had been recently ploughed. By now he knew it was better not to waste his breath on questions that were unlikely to be answered.

After a couple of hundred metres they reached a low

hedge and passed through a three-barred gate into a second field, which was wide and open. Up ahead, Paul could make out the outline of a wooded area, but before they reached it, Louis stopped. A wooden post had been hammered into the ground. A painted sign at head height stated simply: DEMARCATION LINE. DO NOT CROSS@

Paul stared. "Is this it?"

Louis nodded. "This is it." He took a single step past the post and looked back at Paul. "I'm in the Free Zone and you're in Occupied France."

"But there's nothing to stop anyone from crossing."

"For the moment," Louis agreed. "Just a post every so often, and here and there another sign like this. In other places it's different; fences, wire, barriers, guards. And once the Germans get more organized it'll change in remote places like this. But for now we must be thankful for what we have." He laughed. "Or don't have."

Paul shook his head. It was hard to believe that nothing more than a wooden post divided the great nation of France in two. "Where do we go now?"

Louis pointed to the dark woodland lying ahead. "We need to get to the other side; it's still quite a way. Then we'll lay up again until daybreak."

"And then?"

The night was at its darkest now, but even so, Paul could just see the slight smile on Louis's face as he replied. "And then, I hope, there will be a pleasant surprise for you."

* * *

It was more than pleasant; it was the height of luxury. Right then Paul wouldn't have wanted to travel in any other way. He lay back in the hay listening to the horses' hooves and the creaking, iron-rimmed wheels as the wagon made its slow progress away from Occupied France.

They were heading towards Lyon. At a speed of two horsepower, Paul calculated it would take at least a week to reach the city. But their immediate destination was a farm where they would transfer to a car, which would ferry them into the city and the Lyon-Perrache railway station.

That would be later. For the moment, with his aching feet and stiff back, Paul was happy to make the most of his first-ever ride in a haywagon.

The wagon was being driven by an old, pipe-smoking farmer, who had said nothing when he pulled up to collect them soon after first light. He simply nodded to Louis, who nodded back. Once his passengers climbed aboard and were comfortably settled in the hay, he flicked the leather reins a couple of times and the two horses plodded on their way.

Paul and Louis shared the last of the bread and cheese, and as the early autumn sun climbed in the sky, they both dozed off. A truck chugged by in the opposite direction and someone on a bicycle shouted good morning, getting no reply from the farmer. Birds were singing; the sky was cloudless; the horses walked slowly on, and Paul for a while slipped into that blissful state where he wasn't quite certain if he were awake or asleep.

He was soon asleep for real though, and dreaming – another nightmare. Two German soldiers were chasing down his father. Then it wasn't his father, but Paul himself. The Germans were closing in on him and one was raising a submachine-gun. "Halt! Halt or I fire!"

Paul woke with a start. For a few seconds, cushioned in soft hay and staring up at the sky, the dream still vivid, he was totally disorientated. Then he heard a horse snort and stamp its hoof, and everything fell into place. But not quite everything. The wagon had stopped moving. Paul heard an engine and then raised voices.

Cautiously, he sat up. The slight movement was enough to make Louis stir and wake. He yawned loudly and began to speak.

"Where are—?"

Paul moved like a flash, clamping a hand over Louis's mouth and shaking his head urgently.

Realizing that something was not right, Louis nodded. Paul moved his hand away and they strained to hear what was being said. The hay and the high sides of the wagon muffled the voices, but they could tell the farmer was arguing with another man.

They heard hurried footsteps on the road and tensed as someone approached the back of the wagon.

"Louis?"

Louis looked at Paul and shook his head.

"Louis, it's all right. It's me; Georges."

"Georges!" Louis snapped. "Why the hell didn't you say something before?"

"I was trying to explain to my father that he can't take you to the farm. The police are checking vehicles. They've blocked the road up ahead."

The new arrival nodded a greeting to Paul.

"Are they looking for us?" Paul asked.

Georges shook his head. "When I came through they said it was just routine, but you never know. Get in the car, we'd better move fast. I'll take us the back route to Lyon."

In seconds they were off the wagon and into an old Renault. Georges started the ignition and with a crunching of gears which would have made Father Lagarde cringe, the car shot off down a side road.

Paul looked back through rear window. The wagon hadn't moved.

The city of Lyon was huge and even busier than Antwerp. But there was another difference that Paul couldn't quite put his finger on – until he realized it was the absence of German soldiers. He was used to seeing many grey army uniforms in the city squares and streets but here in the Free Zone there were none. It was almost as though the war was not happening.

"I can't stay with you for long," Louis told Paul as they approached the station, "I need to get back to the farm with Georges. If it's safe."

"Will you go home tonight?"

"Maybe," Louis said with a shrug. "You did the right thing in the wagon, shutting me up before I could shoot my mouth off."

"It didn't matter though," Paul said.

"But it might have done. You were alert, aware. You must stay like that all the time now."

Georges stopped the car close to the station, a huge old building, and Paul and Louis got out. Queuing for a ticket to Montpellier took just a few minutes, and then Louis led Paul to a quiet corner where they could speak without being overheard.

"I'll see you through the barrier and then I'll slip away," he said. "And remember, Renard will meet you at Montpellier station. He'll find you and make himself known."

They shook hands. Suddenly Paul was aware that for the remainder of his journey south he would be on his own.

"Thank you," he said, "for everything you've done."

Louis shrugged his shoulders modestly. Then he watched as Paul approached the barrier, where several French police officers stood. He gave his documents to the closest one and waited while they were thoroughly scrutinized.

"Why are you travelling to Montpellier?" the officer asked.

"To work," Paul answered confidently. "My family have friends there; they've offered me a job."

"What sort of job?"

"In a bank; I'm good with figures."

The officer hesitated for a moment before handing back the documents. "Have a good journey." He winked. "And put a few francs into my account when you get there, will you?"

"I'll see what I can do," Paul said with a grin.

He went through the barrier, tucked his documents into the inside pocket of his jacket and then looked back.

There was no sign of Louis; he had slipped away, exactly as he had said he would.

And Paul was alone.

EIGHTEEN

Josette had been in agony since seeing her father and Gaston Rouzard plotting together in the factory office, and as the days passed her despair did not diminish.

She didn't want to believe it, of course, but there was no escaping what she had witnessed: her father, the man she loved and respected above all others, was a collaborator.

There was no one she could speak to. She couldn't talk to her mother; for all Josette knew, her mother might also have turned traitor. She couldn't talk to her grandmother because she couldn't bear to see the anguish the revelation would bring to Odile. And she couldn't talk to Didier Brunet because he had warned her about having anything to do with Jean-Pierre Dilhat, making it perfectly clear that he wouldn't be involved himself.

But Jean-Pierre was in danger. She'd heard Rouzard tell her father they had to do something about him. That could only mean one thing; they were going betray him to the authorities, reveal that he was leading a fledgling Resistance movement in the town. And as a local gendarme officer, Rouzard might be preparing to make the arrest at any moment.

Josette had considered warning Jean-Pierre. But to do that, she would have to admit that her own father was one of the collaborators out to destroy him and the Resistance. She couldn't do it. Not yet. Despite everything, she still loved her father. And love just couldn't turn to hatred in an instant.

But why had a fierce patriot who loved his country suddenly turned traitor? It was inexplicable.

Recalling her grandmother's words, all Josette could think was that the horrors Henri had witnessed in the First World War, coupled with the death of Venant, had led him to decide that nothing was worth fighting and dying for. He simply wanted an end to it, she reasoned. No more war, no more fighting. Even if that meant betraying a young man devoted to the cause of freedom and liberty. In her head it almost made sense, but not in her heart.

She had hardly spoken to her father for the past few days, avoiding him whenever possible. It wasn't easy when they lived in the same house and shared the same workspace. So she was grateful that Henri was out for the day, seeing a raw-material supplier somewhere over in Foix.

Josette was in the office, half-heartedly going through the accounts, unable to focus on her work for more than a few minutes at a time. It was early afternoon and she had not gone home to have lunch with her mother. There would almost certainly have been questions; both parents had noticed how subdued and withdrawn she had been, so unlike her normal self. Up till now she'd fobbed them off, saying she felt unwell. But she couldn't go on making the same excuse.

So here she was, shut in the office, away from everyone and everything. She hadn't even bothered to eat; over the past few days she'd lost her appetite anyway. What did food matter at a time like this?

A large accounts ledger was open on the desk in front of her. As she stared at the figures, they blurred before her eyes. With a sigh, she went back to the top of the row and began to count again.

Suddenly, Josette threw down her pen. It was no good, she had to speak to someone; she was going crazy. She got up from her desk, hurried from the office and down the stairs onto the factory floor.

The racket of the looms and loading machines thundered in her ears. She was going to speak to Didier after all. He would understand. He would tell her what to do.

As she rounded the corner she almost bumped into the factory foreman, Marcel Castelnaud, and one of the loom operators, Yvette Bigou. They were huddled together, deep in conversation, but quickly moved apart as they saw her. The din of the machines prevented Josette from hearing what they'd said, but both looked embarrassed.

Marcel was quickest to recover his composure. He was

a small, neat man in his early fifties, who always had a smile on his face, making him popular with the factory workforce.

"Ah, Josette," he beamed. "Yvette and I were talking about the new order that's come in."

It was an obvious lie, but at that moment Josette just wanted to get to Didier.

Marcel stood in her way, still grinning. "It will mean extra shifts for the girls." He turned to the sour-faced Yvette. "That will keep you all happy, eh, Yvette?"

Josette didn't like Yvette and she knew the feeling was mutual. Yvette was a whiner and a gossip, always ready to dish the dirt. And having worked at the factory for more than twenty years, she liked to strut around as though she owned the place. But Josette's father said Yvette was the best loom operator he had, so he reckoned it was worth putting up with her.

Yvette gave a shrug of indifference, but seeing Josette was waiting for an answer she said reluctantly, "I suppose so."

Civilities were completed and Josette had no desire to prolong the conversation. "I have to speak to Didier," she said quickly, and hurried away before either had the chance to reply.

Didier was in his workshop, hunched over a bench, his face a mask of concentration as he carefully filed at a metal spool, gripped securely in a vice.

"Didier?" Josette called from the doorway.

He didn't respond at first.

"Didier!" Josette called again, much louder.

Didier looked up and nodded. "I thought you'd be here soon enough," he said, putting down the file.

"Why? What do you mean?" Josette said, puzzled.

"Surely you've heard?"

"Heard what?"

Didier moved closer. "Everyone in the factory is talking about it. Makes me sick; they should mind their own business, the lot of them. It was Yvette Bigou who saw it, of course; she was bound to, wasn't she? She just *happened* to be there at the right moment and couldn't wait to get back here to spread the news."

"Didier!" Josette shouted. "Will you please tell me what you're talking about?"

Didier sighed and shook his head. "Jean-Pierre Dilhat has been arrested."

NINETEEN

Paul was being watched. Lyon-Perrache was a major station with a huge, bustling concourse. Yet someone had picked him out from the crowd, he was certain. He could feel eyes boring into him, without being able to spot the watcher.

For a while, he thought it was his imagination, a consequence of being suddenly alone after spending the previous days in such close company. But he soon knew it wasn't his imagination; someone was spying on him.

Paul desperately wanted to get on the train and be on the move again. But he was early; the train had yet to arrive. He had no alternative but to wait and stay alert, like Louis had told him. That included remembering what *not* to do. *Don't stare at people and they won't stare at you. Don't pace about looking anxious. Stay calm and stay quiet.* Sabine and Louis had stressed each of these instructions. But it was almost impossible when he knew someone was eying him.

Slowly he scanned the concourse from side to side. A few

men loitered by coffee stands or near tobacco kiosks; a couple of gendarmes chatted to each other as they strolled leisurely along a platform; porters pushed heavily loaded trolleys. None appeared to be watching him. Or at least, he didn't think so.

He glanced up at the clock and frowned; the train should have arrived by now. Before the war, France had boasted one of Europe's finest railway systems. But the division of the country meant new routes had hastily been drawn up and new timetables implemented on both sides of the Demarcation Line. In some ways it was a miracle any trains were running at all, let alone running on time.

Ten minutes behind schedule, the train drew into the platform and the waiting passengers began to move towards the carriages. Paul hung back; even if the driver wanted to make up lost time, it would be several minutes before departure. He had no intention of making it easy for someone to follow him onto the train.

He bided his time, letting the minutes tick by. Carriage doors slammed shut, platform staff shouted and eventually a whistle sounded from somewhere further down the platform.

Just before the train started to move, Paul sprang forward, running the few metres to one of the last open carriage doors. He leapt up onto the steps and at the same time noticed a movement further along the train to his right. He saw no one but heard a door slam, and knew instinctively that his pursuer had jumped aboard.

* * *

There were plenty of empty seats. Paul moved along the corridor, getting closer to the front before choosing a half-full compartment. He placed his case on the rack and settled into his seat, still wondering if he should have stayed in the corridor and waited. But what was the point? He wouldn't know his pursuer if he saw him. Or her. All he could do was sit tight and stay vigilant.

After a while, with the train ploughing steadily southward, he began to wonder again if perhaps he had imagined it all. A few people passed by in the corridor but no one gave more than a quick glance into the compartment.

An elderly couple sat opposite. Paul watched as the woman lifted a straw basket from the floor onto the man's lap. She delved inside and brought out most of a baguette, some thick, fatty sausage and something wrapped in white paper. As she unwrapped it the pungent smell of over-ripe cheese filled the compartment.

No one but Paul seemed remotely concerned; a passenger by the door even smiled and nodded his approval as the heavy odour clogged the air. Paul felt like gagging. He forced himself to sit back and gaze out of the window, his thoughts flying immediately back to the station at Lyon and the feeling that someone had been watching him. Perhaps, he reflected, his mind was too full of intrigue and suspicion. It wasn't surprising; he'd experienced little else for days.

At Valance, the second station stop, the elderly couple

departed, leaving behind them the lingering aroma of old cheese. One by one the other passengers left too, and by the time the train began its long haul down to Avignon, the sun was setting and Paul was alone in the compartment.

The travelling, the hours of tense waiting, and a mind crammed with unanswered questions were all taking their toll. And new questions were running through his brain. Had his father been a spy? Were his visits to the German harbours really necessary or were they part of an elaborate plan drawn up in preparation for the war many in Europe had feared long before it actually came? And then there was his mother. Was she a spy too? Paul sighed. All these questions would remain unanswered unless he was reunited with her.

As the train chugged onward and his thoughts tumbled one on top of the other, Paul realized that another emotion, gnawing away deep inside for days, had finally surfaced. He was angry. Angry at what had happened to his parents, certainly, but angry *towards* his parents too. They had lied and deliberately kept him from the truth, while secretly making plans for the family's escape to England. Not a word to Paul. Hadn't he, at very least, deserved to know that his life was about to change so completely? And now his father was dead and his mother quite possibly dead. Somehow – he didn't yet understand why – he was angry with them for that too. For getting killed, for getting snatched away.

Paul was weary; the hypnotic rhythm of the train's wheels lulled him towards sleep. His eyelids grew heavy.

His head began to nod, his eyes closing.

Suddenly, the compartment's sliding door crashed back and Paul snapped into consciousness, his eyes wide open. He had to stay awake and alert. Had to. A man wearing a trilby hat and an overcoat stood in the doorway. He was around forty, thin-faced and a little taller than Paul.

Paul knew instantly that his pursuer had arrived.

"Good evening," the man said, smiling and raising his hat. "I'm sorry if I startled you. The compartment I was in was rather noisy. Do you mind if I join you?"

Paul shrugged. "It's not my train."

The man laughed and Paul instantly regretted his flippant comment. He should have said nothing, kept himself to himself, as he'd been instructed.

"If it were yours perhaps you'd get it running on time again, eh?" the man said, sliding the door shut and taking a seat opposite Paul.

This time Paul didn't reply, but turned instead to look out of the window.

"Where are you travelling to?" the man asked, seemingly determined to start a conversation.

"If you don't mind," Paul said, turning back, "I'm very tired. I've had a long day."

"Of course, of course, I shouldn't have woken you, barging in the way I did. You sleep, I'll just sit here quietly and I won't disturb you again."

Paul nodded and closed his eyes.

But he didn't sleep; there was no way he could sleep now.

The door slid back again and Paul opened his eyes.

"Papers and tickets, please," said the train guard, stepping into the compartment.

As he checked the other man's papers Paul thought he saw the two men exchange a slight glance of recognition. The guard gave both passengers' documents no more than a fleeting look before handing them back and leaving the carriage. It might have meant nothing, but it increased Paul's suspicions.

"It seems no one will let you sleep," the man said with a smile that was somehow menacing.

Paul responded with a nod and a half smile of his own, attempting to cut dead any conversation before it began. But the attempt was in vain.

"My name is Lucien Galtier," the man continued. "And you are?"

"Paul, Paul Héroux."

"Very nice to meet you, Paul. May I call you Paul?"

Paul nodded.

"Where are you travelling to, Paul?"

"Montpellier."

"Ah, me too. Do you live in Montpellier?"

"No."

"Visiting friends? Relatives?"

"No."

Galtier stared, head tilted slightly to one side, smile fixed as he waited, wordlessly demanding further explanation.

"I'm hoping to get a job," Paul said finally. "In a bank. I'm good with figures." *Too much information*, he told himself. *Far too much.*

"How fortunate to be good with figures," Galtier said. "I'm afraid I never was. And is this bank you're hoping to work at in Montpellier? I may know it."

"No, it's not in Montpellier."

Once again, Galtier stared and smiled, awaiting more information.

"It's … it's in a small town, near Foix."

"Ah, I know that area. Which town?"

It was one question too many.

"Why are you asking me all these questions?" Paul snapped.

Galtier's smile did not fade for a moment. "Just making conversation. These train journeys can be so tedious, don't you think?"

"No, I don't think that," Paul said, trying not to lose his temper. "I enjoy train journeys; they give me time to think. But if you don't mind, I'm tired, and I'm not in the mood for talking."

"As you wish," Galtier said, calmly. He paused for a moment before continuing in the same friendly, persuasive manner. "It's not too long before we reach Avignon. We stop there for a little while, there's time to get out and stretch your legs and get some fresh air. It will make you feel better."

"I don't need to feel better," Paul said curtly. "I'm not unwell, just tired, that's all."

Galtier nodded, but said no more.

Paul looked away, not knowing what to do but aware that he was being played like a fish on a line.

TWENTY

Paul forced himself not to look in Galtier's direction for the remainder of the journey to Avignon. It wasn't easy; he could feel Galtier's eyes on him, calculating, assessing, plotting his next move.

And all the while Paul was trying to work out his own next move. He considered leaving the train at Avignon and waiting there for the next one to Montpellier. But he had no idea when the next train would be or even if there was another that night.

Besides, the mysterious Renard would be waiting at Montpellier to meet this train; Paul had to stay on board and see the journey through.

He thought about moving to another compartment or another carriage. But that would only increase Galtier's suspicions and there was nothing to stop him following or observing from a distance. At least when they were in the same compartment Paul knew where Galtier was. In the end he decided to sit tight. Hopefully Renard would have a contingency plan for an emergency situation like this. Hopefully.

The train slowed and then jolted to a standstill. They had reached Avignon.

Galtier got to his feet. "I think I will take a little stroll and get some air. Will you join me, Paul?"

"No, thanks. I'll stay here."

Galtier smiled his menacing smile. "As you wish."

He didn't go far. Paul could see him on the platform, standing beneath the dim, yellow station lamps, smoking a cigarette. Every so often his eyes would flick back to the compartment, checking that Paul was still in his seat. He smoked one cigarette and then immediately lit another, exchanging a few words with another man who passed by. There was little other movement on the platform; no one seemed in much of a hurry to get the train back on schedule.

Eventually a whistle sounded and carriage doors began to slam. Galtier didn't move. He took a long drag at his cigarette, turned towards Paul and then smiled and waved, almost as though he were bidding him goodbye.

The train began to move, edging away very slowly. Still Galtier didn't stir. He disappeared from view and Paul instantly felt as though a huge weight was lifting from his shoulders. *He didn't get back on*, he said to himself. *He's given up; decided I'm not worth bothering with after all.*

He stared at the deserted corridor, needing to be certain; but there was no one. Finally, with a long sigh of relief, he let his head fall back against the headrest and stared up at the ceiling.

And then the door glided back and Galtier was there.

"Such a terrible habit, smoking, isn't it? I always have to get the last possible puff. Nearly missed getting back on board. I don't suppose you smoke, do you?"

Paul shook his head, disappointment surging through his entire body.

"Very sensible," Galtier said. "Very, very sensible."

Paul stood up. He had to get away. He felt certain now that if he got off the train with Galtier at Montpellier, he would be taken into custody and interrogated.

"Going somewhere?" Galtier asked as he moved towards the door.

"I have to. If that's all right with you."

"Ah, yes, of course. It's down at the end of the carriage, to your left."

Without another word, Paul pushed back the door and went into the corridor. He stood for a moment, staring through the window into the dark night. Then he saw Galtier's face reflected in the glass, watching him, as he had been for hours.

Paul yanked the door shut. Galtier simply smiled and nodded, and Paul had the sudden urge to punch his smug, leering face. Instead, he walked quickly down the corridor, past the lavatory compartment and through the door at the end of the carriage.

Outside, he stood on the metal walkway, where just a thin handrail on either side separated him from the rails below.

The noise of the wheels thundering over the track and the night air rushing by gave an indication of the train's breakneck speed. But the cold air did little to cool Paul's temper; the anger that had been fermenting for days was ready to boil over. He sucked in several deep breaths, knowing he had to channel that rage, keep it under control and think clearly.

The walkway was no place to linger – he had to do something. So he went through the door into the next carriage and continued all the way along the corridor, passing mainly empty compartments, to the next outside walkway.

He stopped again and stared down into the darkness, wondering for a moment if he might risk jumping. Then he would somehow find his way to Montpellier. But rocking from side to side on the narrow walkway was enough to convince Paul that a leap into the unknown would almost certainly be suicidal.

"Not thinking of leaving the train early, are you, Paul?"

Paul hadn't even heard Galtier approach. He turned and met his stare.

The smile had finally disappeared and in his right hand, pointed at Paul's chest, was a small pistol.

"Please don't consider jumping, Paul, it would be most unwise. I doubt very much if you'd survive and I do want to talk to you seriously when we reach Montpellier." He gestured with the pistol. "Let's go back to our compartment. You lead the way."

Paul didn't panic now that Galtier had finally made his move. He felt stronger, despite the pistol. "Who are you?" he asked.

"You know who I am. Lucien Galtier. It's you who's of interest. Somehow I don't think your name really is Paul Héroux."

"Are you the police?"

"No, I'm not police."

"Then why should I do as you say?"

Galtier's malevolent smile returned. "Because, firstly, I work for our government, hunting down escapees like you and, secondly, I have a loaded pistol pointed at your heart."

"But you won't shoot me," Paul replied coolly.

Standing in the darkness, facing each other on the narrow walkway as the train rocked from side to side, Paul thought that, for the first time, he glimpsed a trace of uncertainty flicker across his pursuer's face.

"Let's not waste any more time," Galtier murmured. "Move, now."

The train was steaming around a long bend, causing the walkway to rock more violently. As it gave a sudden shudder, Paul quickly gripped the side rails with both hands. Galtier could only snatch at one rail because of the pistol.

The walkway jolted with force and Galtier staggered,

toppling forwards. He crashed into Paul and grabbed his jacket in an attempt to recover his balance.

In that instant the pistol went spinning from his hand and disappeared into the night.

Galtier clung on tightly, and Paul knew that he had a chance. He drew back his right arm and punched Galtier in the gut, making him gasp and almost double up. They were close in height and build, but Paul was strong for his age and had seized the initiative with the first blow.

And he was angry. Furious.

Instinctively he followed up his first punch with a swinging left, which smashed into Galtier's ear. Galtier's yell was full of rage. He clawed at Paul's throat, managing to get both hands around his neck.

Paul reached up and grabbed Galtier's fingers, attempting to rip his hands away. But Galtier gripped tighter, pressing his fingers deep into Paul's flesh, throttling, squeezing his windpipe, making his eyes bulge as he struggled for air.

Paul felt his lungs burning as Galtier's hold tightened. His smile had returned, malevolent once more, and his eyes were darkening in triumph.

Paul was weakening with every second, close to losing consciousness. A desperate thought flashed across his mind. He instantly let go of the hands at his throat and grasped both side rails. Then, with a final effort, he drew back a leg and drove his knee fiercely into Galtier's groin.

Galtier's yell was pure agony as he released his two-handed grip on Paul's throat. Paul swung his right arm. There was little power in the punch this time, but his fist connected perfectly with Galtier's face, sending him reeling.

A single scream – pain mixed with terror – pierced the air as Galtier crashed over the rail and plunged downwards through the gap between the carriages.

And then there was nothing but the roar of the train as it hurtled on through the darkness.

TWENTY-ONE

The face that stared back at Paul in the compartment window seemed like the face of a total stranger. But the haunted eyes and haggard features were his own, almost unrecognizable from those of the sixteen-year-old boy of a week earlier. This boy was older, changed for ever.

Every few minutes Paul glanced towards the corridor, expecting the sliding door to open and for Galtier to be standing there, grinning that evil grin, having miraculously survived the fall from the train.

But Paul knew no miracle had happened. There was no chance that Galtier could have recovered from the plunge onto the track and the vicious, turning wheels. His end would have been swift and terrible.

Paul's body ached – his fists hurt, his neck throbbed and his throat was raw, as if he had been swallowing glass. But beyond the physical pain there was something else, something he was struggling to understand. He felt better, deep inside. He wasn't proud at being responsible for the death of another person, but finally, after days of obediently following orders, having every moment of his life organized by others, he had stood up for himself. He had fought his own battle. He had fought for his life. And survived.

The shriek of the engine's whistle brought back the memory of Galtier's final scream, and Paul shivered. He shook his head and forced himself to look past his reflection. Outside there were lights in the darkness; the train was slowing as it reached the outskirts of Montpellier.

Drained and weary, Paul got up and lifted down his suitcase from the rack. He was still in danger. It was possible that Galtier had been expected at Montpellier. Perhaps when he had spoken to the man on Avignon station he was sending a message onwards; perhaps gendarme officers were waiting on the platform at that very moment to take him into custody.

There were too many possibilities to plan for. For the moment Paul had to focus on getting to Renard. He would know what to do.

The train shuddered to a halt and Paul climbed down from the carriage. He strode, not too quickly, along the platform. *Don't stare at people and they won't stare at you. Don't look anxious. Stay calm; stay quiet.*

It was late. The station kiosks were closed and darkened. Few people were about, and Paul was relieved to note the absence of any gendarme officers. The other passengers filed past, one or two greeted by waiting friends or relatives, but Paul could spot no one who seemed remotely interested in him. He wasn't surprised; Renard was obviously being cautious, waiting to see if Paul was being followed.

He reached the main ticket area and lingered for a moment, giving Renard the chance to recognize him, before strolling slowly over to a closed kiosk. He watched the last passengers leave the building.

The train was going no further; the engine was shut down; the driver, fireman and guard had sauntered away from the platform and an eerie silence had descended over the station.

Seconds turned to minutes. Paul gazed around once more. The station was empty. And then he realized: Renard wasn't coming.

Montpellier looked almost ready for sleep. The cobbled streets outside the station were virtually free of traffic. A young couple hurried homeward on the far pavement, the woman's high-heeled footsteps echoing in the still air. Across the way, lights burned dimly in the window of one of the few cafés still open for business.

From the station entrance, Paul could see clearly into the café. It was deserted, save for the barman washing glasses to the recorded strains of a melancholy female voice and an accordion.

The song ended; the barman didn't bother changing the record.

There was no curfew here in the Free Zone, but few people were demonstrating any enthusiasm for a late night out.

Paul turned to his right and walked away from the station, sticking to the shadows where he could. Going this way was a random decision, it just seemed important to get clear of the station. It was a major city building, a landmark, and patrolling gendarme officers were likely to turn up at any moment, for routine checks if nothing else.

As he walked and more of the city revealed itself, Paul was reminded of parts of Antwerp. The wide boulevards, large shop fronts and pavement cafés, their tables and chairs now stacked and huddled under awnings, brought back fleeting memories of the city he loved so much. And the people he loved too.

But there was no point now in thinking about Antwerp and the past. Paul was in trouble; he had to decide what to do. And he was concerned about Renard. Could he have been captured and arrested? Or worse, injured or killed? Was it possible that the unknown traitor in Antwerp had managed to inform on the Resistance group in distant Lavelanet?

Paul was worried but he wasn't panicking. After the fight on the train, he didn't think he would ever feel panic again. But he knew no one in Montpellier, indeed in the whole of southern France. He had hardly any money, probably not enough for a night in a hotel – and even if he could find cheap lodging, questions would be asked and papers checked. A suspicious hotelier with the wrong sympathies might very well call the police.

But being alone and so visible on the city streets was too dangerous; sooner or later Paul was certain to be stopped. And besides, he was desperately tired; he had to sleep, and soon. If only he could get a few hours he knew he'd think more clearly.

He'd noticed what looked like a small park across the road from the station – or, if not a park, definitely some trees and grass. And if there were trees and grass there were bound to be benches. The night was warm and Paul decided he would find a bench to curl up on.

He turned and started to retrace his steps. He had walked in virtually a straight line from the station. He smiled ruefully, thinking, *At least it's not raining.*

Within a few minutes he was approaching the station again. As he drew nearer, he saw a man leave the building and stop outside the entrance.

Paul halted, pressing his back against a wall, trying to be invisible. Maybe it was one of Galtier's contacts, concerned that he had not reported in after the arrival of the Lyon train.

Then again, perhaps it was Renard?

The man was staring out into the streets, obviously searching for someone.

Paul eased himself away from the wall and edged cautiously forward, seeking out the shadows with every hesitant step.

He was close enough now to see that the man had his right elbow cupped in his left hand. His chin was resting in his right hand and he was rhythmically stroking a bushy moustache with his right index finger.

Paul decided he had to take the risk. He stepped out from the shadows, and as he did the man turned in his direction, stared and came hurrying towards him. "Paul?" he asked quickly. "Are you Paul?"

Paul hesitated, reluctant to admit to his own identity until he was certain about the man. "Are you … are you…?" His bruised vocal chords had turned his voice into little more than a hoarse croak. "I'm sorry. Are you…?"

"Renard?" The man grinned. "Yes, I'm Renard."

Paul nodded, relief flooding through his body. "And I'm Paul."

TWENTY-TWO

Henri was not expecting a welcoming committee when he arrived home with Paul, but that was exactly what he got.

As the door swung open, he was greeted by his wife, Hélène; his daughter, Josette; Didier Brunet, and the gendarme officer, Gaston Rouzard.

All four advanced along the hallway, but Josette was first to reach Henri, hurling herself across the tiles and into his arms.

"I'm sorry, Papa. I'm so, so, sorry," she said tearfully. "I should never have doubted you. Or Didier, or Gaston. I should never have doubted any of you. Never, never, never!"

Lost for words, Henri gazed over Josette's shoulder to the others.

Didier wore a guilty look on his face. He raised both hands, palms upward and shrugged apologetically. "I had to tell her. I tried not to, but she was convinced you and Gaston were traitors, and responsible for Jean-Pierre Dilhat being arrested."

"Arrested?" Henri said, freeing himself from Josette's clinging arms and easing her away. "Jean-Pierre has been arrested?"

Gaston Rouzard took up the story. "Of course, you wouldn't have heard. It seems our warnings to take care came too late. He was taken today. There was nothing I could do to stop it."

"Where have they taken him?" Henri asked.

"I don't know," Rouzard said, with a shake of his head. "But I'll find out."

Hélène stepped over to Henri and took one of his hands in hers. "You're so late. We were all terribly worried. What happened?"

"I know, I'm sorry," Henri answered, smiling at his wife and squeezing her hand. "That idiot Maurice, over at Foix, kept me waiting for hours. I should have known; he's always late. And then it took far longer to reach Montpellier than I thought it would. It's changed so much since the last time I was there. By the time I found the station and left the car, I was late myself. Then I went into the station and there was no sign of Paul, and … oh…"

Henri remembered suddenly that Paul was behind him. He turned and held out a welcoming hand of introduction.

"I'm so sorry," he said. "Everyone, this is our new friend, Paul."

Paul had been standing, suitcase in hand, in the open doorway, attempting – and failing – to figure out who they all were and what exactly was going on. He was exhausted and in a lot of pain. He felt dizzy and hot, and waves of tiredness and nausea were washing over him.

Four faces smiled expectantly.

Paul smiled back. "Hello," he croaked.

And then everything went black as he collapsed onto the cold tiles.

"Is he a bit soft?" Josette asked her father.

It was lunchtime the following day and there was so much she needed to know and had, until now, been unable to ask.

"No, he certainly is *not* soft," Henri said, cutting a slice of cheese. "From what I learned last night he's a very brave young man."

"But he fainted," Josette said, with more than a hint of scorn in her voice. "That's soft. There's nothing in the world that would make me faint," conveniently forgetting that she had almost fainted when she heard her father and Gaston Rouzard talking in the office.

"He's been through some terrible experiences," Henri said, "including seeing his own father shot dead."

Hélène stared at her husband. "He told you this?"

Henri nodded. "And last night, another man—" He stopped himself from continuing.

"Another man, what?" Josette asked quickly.

Henri shook his head. "It doesn't matter."

"More secrets, Papa?"

"There are some things it's best you don't know."

"Well, I don't agree. How long have you known he was coming here?"

"About a week."

"And were you going to tell me? Or was I meant to get up this morning to find him sitting here eating breakfast?"

"I was going to tell you, Josette, when it was first arranged. Remember the day you were late home for lunch? I planned to tell you then. But you came storming in with all this wild talk of resistance and taking action; it worried me. You're so impulsive, and that's dangerous. Then the last few days we've hardly spoken; there never seemed to be the right moment."

"But, Papa—"

Henri cut the argument short, taking the knife again and carefully slicing a thin sliver of cheese. When he looked up he saw Hélène staring at the photograph of Venant. He sighed. He was uncomfortably aware that Paul's presence in the house and the loss of his father would only heighten Hélène's feelings of grief for their own son. "We must give Paul time to recover," he told her gently. "How was he when you took up the soup?"

"Awake," she answered. "A little confused. He said he would come down."

"And what did you say?"

"That he should rest. But I certainly can't tell him what to do; he's not a child."

"I fear that by the time this war ends there will be no children at all," said Henri. "War makes even the young old."

They sat without speaking for a few moments, each lost in their own thoughts, until Josette, as she frequently did, broke the silence. "Papa, I am sorry I doubted you. I should never have believed you were anything but a true patriot."

"Like you?" Henri said, smiling.

"Of course like me. And I'm so relieved about Gaston and Didier. Please tell me what it is you're doing – and how Jean-Pierre Dilhat is involved?"

"Josette, as I said, it's best that you don't know—"

"Papa, please! We're all in this together and I want to help!"

"No!" Henri said, louder than he intended. He lowered his voice. "It may become dangerous."

"I don't care about the danger."

"But I do! You're my daughter, and I've already lost my..." Henri turned his head away and silence filled the room again.

Hélène reached across the table and put a hand on one of Henri's. "Tell her what you're doing," she said softly. "She should know."

Henri took a deep, halting breath, almost like a sob. Then he sighed and turned to his daughter. "There is little we can do at the moment; there are no Germans here for us to fight like there are in the north. But that may change. Mostly, for now, we're making contact with others, trying to become more organized, waiting to do something useful. Now we have our chance. Very soon, we're going to help Paul escape across the mountains into Spain."

Josette considered her father's words. "And what about Jean-Pierre?"

"We are few in number; Jean-Pierre has been trying to recruit more. But, as has been proved, it's difficult to know who can be trusted. And Jean-Pierre ... well, Jean-Pierre is like you, a bit of a hothead. But he's a good man, and we must do what we can for him."

Josette turned to her mother. "Did you know all this?"
Hélène nodded.

"And Gra-mere? Does she know?"

"I'm going to see her tomorrow," Henri said. "I'll explain, but I'd be surprised if she doesn't have a pretty good idea already. Your grandmother doesn't miss much."

They heard the sound of creaking stair treads in the hallway.

"Paul," Henri said quietly.

The door opened slowly. Paul looked pale and washed-out. There were dark bruises around his neck.

Nevertheless Henri said, "Ah, Paul, you look much better," trying to sound encouraging. "Do come in and sit with us."

Paul sat down in the chair next to Hélène. Henri glanced at his wife and saw the sadness in her eyes. It was the chair Venant always used.

But Hélène smiled at Paul. "Could you manage some bread and cheese? There's still plenty."

"You're very kind," Paul croaked. "But, no thank you."

Josette stared. "What's wrong with your voice?" she asked, as blunt as ever.

"Josette, please!" Henri said. "All these questions, all the time."

"I only asked about his—"

"Enough, Josette!"

Josette shrugged and was silent.

"We didn't manage proper introductions last night, Paul," Henri said, "but you met my wife, Hélène, earlier, and this extremely inquisitive person is our daughter, Josette. Please don't feel you have to answer all, or indeed any, of her questions."

"All I did was asked about his voice, it's—"

"Yes, thank you, Josette."

Josette sighed and gave a slight nod of acknowledgement to Paul.

"We'll talk about our plans as soon as you're a little stronger, Paul," Henri continued, "but in the meantime is there anything you want to know?"

"Not really," Paul said. He swallowed, his throat feeling even more raw than it had the previous evening. "Except...'

"Yes?"

"I was wondering," he managed to mumble, "about your code-name, Renard?"

"Renard!" Josette said, her eyes wide with amazement. "I didn't know you were called Renard!"

Henri smiled. "It's simple really. Old Maurice over at Foix, he says I'm a wily old fox when it comes to negotiating a price. So, when I had to choose a code-name, I decided on Renard."

"You see!" Josette snapped, looking highly put out. "You tell him, but you didn't tell me. You never tell me anything!"

TWENTY-THREE

A watery sun was dropping towards the mountains and there was a distinct chill in the air, but Paul was grateful to be out of the house at last.

He had remained indoors for a further two days as the bruises on his neck turned from brown to a dirty yellow. Henri worried that such highly visible marks would arouse suspicion in the town and said it was safest for Paul to recover his strength in the house while the bruising faded.

He stayed mainly in his room, reading a little and thinking a lot, especially about his life-or-death struggle with Galtier. He had no regrets. It had been him or his pursuer, and Paul began to think of it as a sort of revenge for the slaughter of his father.

Henri and Hélène Mazet had been kind and sympathetic. But Paul didn't want sympathy; he wanted to know what would happen next, when his journey over the mountains would begin. So far, he'd been told nothing.

Josette attempted to draw him into conversation whenever she could, desperate to learn more than her father had revealed. But Paul remained evasive and, Josette decided, deliberately elusive; he made excuses to get away or, when she had him cornered, did ridiculous mimes meant to suggest that his throat was too sore for him to speak.

Josette was never slow in reaching an opinion on a person, and after three days she had decided that Paul was a snob, and that she didn't like him.

But at lunch on the third day, when Paul complained that he had to get out for some fresh air, Josette was quick to offer a late-afternoon tour of the town. After some resistance, her father relented, but insisted that Paul wear a scarf around his neck to hide the bruises.

The tour didn't take very long; there wasn't a great deal to see. Three main streets, with smaller streets running off them, a central area where the market was held, the normal range of shops, a cinema and the river. There was also a small railway station, but Paul had had enough of stations and trains for a while.

It felt good to be outside and to see for the first time the closest peaks of the mighty Pyrenees. Having spent most of his life in England and the flatlands of Belgium, Paul had never been this close to real mountains. They were an awesome sight, dark and brooding, even in the late sun, and a constant reminder of the crossing he had to make if he was to reach England and safety.

He was still feeling disorientated and a bit bewildered, which was partly why he said very little in response to Josette's almost constant chatter and endless questions. But his throat was better and his voice more or less back to normal.

They were on a small side street, heading back to the house, when Paul suddenly stopped.

"What *is* that noise?"

"What noise?" Josette replied tersely.

"That sort of ... wait ... there, you must hear it, that clicking and humming. A mechanical noise."

"Oh, that. It's a loom."

Paul looked up and down the street. It was lined on both sides with small houses. "I don't see a factory."

Josette shrugged. "Many people have looms in their homes. Children learn how to operate them when they're young, so everyone takes a turn and they hardly ever stop. It's said that wherever you go in Lavelanet you can hear the sound of the looms."

"Doesn't the noise drive you mad?"

Josette laughed. "You wait until you get to the factory," she said. "That's proper noise."

Paul nodded and started to walk again. "Maybe that's why everyone here speaks so loudly."

"What do you mean?" Josette said, her eyes darkening.

"I noticed it when we bought the bread, and in the other shop where you got the cheese. Everyone speaks so loudly.

And the accent here is very…" he paused to find the right word *"…harsh."*

Paul hadn't meant to be critical; he was simply trying to say that the strong accent of south-west France was different from anything he had previously heard. But he didn't know Josette well enough to watch what he said; he had yet to experience her fiery temper.

Josette stopped and grabbed Paul's arm. "Oh, so we're too loud and you don't like our harsh accent. Anything else?"

"No, I didn't say I didn't like it. I said—"

"I suppose you think you're better than us."

"I didn't say that either, and I—"

"With your fancy Parisian accent!"

"I've never been to Paris."

"Just because we sound different, it doesn't mean we're not as good as you."

"I know that," Paul said, realizing too late that he should have chosen his words more carefully. "I'm not used to your accent, that's all, and some of the words you use are different."

"Oh, I see. We haven't learned to speak properly either," Josette snapped sarcastically. "Well, I'm sorry we don't know as many clever words as you. Maybe it's because we're busy working out the best way to save your life! And at least I've got something to say; you've said next to nothing since you arrived!"

Paul looked around. The street was deserted but that didn't mean no one was listening. "I've learned to keep my mouth shut," he hissed, "unless there's something that needs to be said." He glanced around again. A door had opened a little further down the street and a woman was peering in their direction. He moved closer to Josette. "Look, I'm sorry, I didn't mean to upset you, but don't you think you should be more careful about what you say too?"

Josette glared, but lowered her voice. "I think I'll go home now; I wouldn't want you to have to listen to my *harsh* voice any more than you absolutely have to!"

She swept away like a whirlwind, leaving Paul staring after her.

Henri Mazet and Gaston Rouzard were sitting beneath the pergola built onto the back wall of the house. The late sunlight, squeezing through the gaps in the tangled vine, was still providing warmth and casting a golden sheen on the stonework.

Henri poured a small amount of pastis into two narrow glasses and then filled them almost to the brim from a jug of water, instantly turning the liquid a dull, milky yellow.

The men lifted their glasses and offered each other a silent toast before sipping their drinks.

"And there's no doubt," Henri asked, "that he's definitely in the Rivel camp?"

"No doubt at all," Gaston replied, replacing his glass on

the table. "And worse than that, he's already said too much and been put into solitary confinement. The conditions in that cell are not good by all accounts, not good at all."

"How long must he stay in there?"

"A few days, my contact says, if he behaves. But that camp is the worst possible place for someone like Jean-Pierre; he won't keep his mouth shut. He'll stir up trouble among the other prisoners and make it even worse for himself."

The two friends gazed out onto the large walled garden, almost bare now save for a few roses here and there. On the trees, leaves were already changing colour and starting to drop.

"And my contact also tells me," Gaston continued, "that pretty soon, the camp at Rivel will be emptied and everyone there will be transferred to Algeria. They'll stick them in camps over there and leave them to rot until the end of the war. We'll probably never see Jean-Pierre again."

Henri considered this for a few moments. "Why is the camp at Rivel being emptied?"

Gaston shrugged his broad shoulders and shook his head. "The rumour is that it's to make room for the large number of Jews they're expecting."

"And who knows where those poor souls will be shipped off to when their turn comes," Henri said, sighing. "When is this to happen?"

"Not long. A few months, maybe less; it could be weeks. No one has been told yet."

The sun finally dipped behind the mountains and the evening was suddenly colder.

Henri finished his drink. "You know what I think?"

Gaston picked up his own glass and drained it. "Tell me?"

"We have four weeks at most to get Paul across the mountains into Spain. After that we can't depend on the weather."

"Agreed," Gaston said, nodding. "But what has that to do with Jean-Pierre?"

"Because when Paul goes," Henri said determinedly, "Jean-Pierre Dilhat is going with him."

TWENTY-FOUR

Paul watched as Henri gently stroked his bushy moustache with the index finger of his right hand. They were seated at the table in Henri's dining room, along with Didier Brunet and Gaston Rouzard. Henri looked concerned, and Paul wondered if he was preparing to deliver bad news. But after a few moments he smiled and placed both hands on the table.

"Well, Paul," he said, "we think it's only right that you know our plan, which has changed a little because of unforeseen circumstances."

Paul nodded, eager to hear the plan, even if it had changed.

"To begin with," Henri continued, "for everyone's safety, it was not my intention that you meet all the members of our group here in Lavelanet. My daughter's vivid imagination changed that part."

Josette, much to her frustration, had been excluded from the discussion and ordered from the room when Didier and Gaston had arrived. But she was resourceful as well as

174

determined. Her bedroom was directly above the dining room and she had long ago learned that if she lay on the floor with one ear pressed flat against a gap in the oak boards she could hear most of what was being said in the room below.

Now she was doing just that, and scowling at her father's comment. "He should have told me the truth in the first place," she murmured.

In the room below, Paul was considering Henri's remark about meeting all the members of the Lavelanet Resistance group. "All?" he said to Henri. "You mean, this is it? There's just three of you?"

Gaston Rouzard gave a philosophical shrug of his broad shoulders. "It's early days and I have a strong feeling this will be a long war. There will be more of us, many more."

"And there was…" Henri stopped to correct himself. "There *is* … one more. Jean-Pierre Dilhat. But as you know, he's been arrested. We've learned that he's being held at an internment camp not far from here; a place called Rivel."

In the room above, Josette gasped.

"It's always been the plan to get you across the mountains to Spain and then to England," Henri told Paul. "There are men living in the mountains, French patriots like us, who will lead you across. Our contacts tell us they are reliable and trustworthy."

Gaston grunted. "And they charge plenty for their services."

"They're taking a huge risk," Henri said. "And, anyway, what's the point of my owning a factory if I don't make good use of the money it brings in?" He turned back to Paul. "A friend in Foix is in contact with them and will let me know when they are ready to make the crossing. Now, this is where our original plan changes…"

Henri's voice dropped, and as Paul leaned closer, in the room above, Josette pressed her ear harder to the floor-boards, straining to pick up what was being said.

"We're going to get Jean-Pierre out."

Paul couldn't stop himself from asking, "But how will you do that?"

Gaston took over. "I have a contact on the inside; he will help. For money, of course."

"And that's as much as you need to know, Paul," Henri said. "Except that when you cross the mountains, Jean-Pierre will be going with you."

"To Spain?" Paul asked.

Henri shook his head. "To England."

"England? Why England?"

"You know of General de Gaulle, of course?"

Paul had a vague recollection of hearing the name at some time, but nothing more than that. "I … I'm not sure."

Didier had been silent until then, but now he clicked his tongue in irritation at Paul's ignorance. "He's our greatest soldier, one of the few to give the Germans a taste of their own medicine before our surrender. Surely you've heard of the battles at Montcornet and Abbeville?"

"I'm sorry, no," Paul replied, his face reddening.

Henri lifted a hand to stop Didier from continuing. "It doesn't really matter," he said. "The point is that he rejected France's surrender and escaped to England. Now he's organizing a new French army over there, preparing to fight when the time comes. As it will be impossible for Jean-Pierre to stay here after his escape, we are sending him to England to join de Gaulle's Free French Forces."

Gaston laughed. "And if I know Jean-Pierre, he'll be telling them all what to do within a few weeks, even the General himself."

"All this will take a little while to organize, Paul," Henri continued, "and we can't keep you shut away here all that time. People will start asking questions. So for now you're coming to work at the factory. If anyone asks – and some are bound to – our families have been friends for years and you're here to learn the business, to see if you like it. When you disappear we'll spread the story that you couldn't settle and have gone home."

Paul sat back; there was a lot to take in. "But what will I actually do?"

Didier leaned across the table. "You're going to be my assistant."

TWENTY-FIVE

The noise was like rolling thunder or a tumultuous water-fall. Paul had no idea how the factory workers coped with it every day. He felt as though his head would explode with the din of looms and loaders and winders. It was deafening. No wonder everyone in Lavelanet shouted most of the time.

Paul's arrival at the factory that first morning had caused quite a stir and set tongues wagging. Not that he'd heard much of what was being said over the constant racket of the machines.

Dressed in a pair of blue overalls, he accompanied his new boss, Didier, on a tour of the factory floor, gazing in awe at the machines, all constantly in motion. Many of them resembled old war machines.

Didier explained the function of each one and Paul heard only a fraction of what was said. He felt like telling Didier he needn't bother with so much detail as he wasn't going to be at the factory for long. But Didier was obviously proud of his machines, so Paul did his best to listen and understand. And when he couldn't quite hear, he nodded seriously, or shook his head, or raised his eyebrows to signify he was impressed, hoping each time he was giving the right response.

The smells of the factory were as powerful and overwhelming as the sounds. Pungent aromas of plant extracts cooking in huge open vats to make dye were heavy in the air.

After an hour Paul was relieved to return to Didier's workshop. But there was no time to settle.

"Do you think you can you find your way around now?" Didier asked.

"Yes, I think so. But my ears are buzzing."

Didier smiled. "You'll get used to it. Take a walk to the loading bay, tell Erneste I'll be over this afternoon to check out the machine that's running hot."

The loading bay was on the far side of the factory. The brief errand should have taken Paul five minutes at the most, but after more than ten he had still not returned. Didier wasn't worried; his new assistant would be back in due course.

Paul was experiencing his first encounter with Yvette Bigou. She had been questioning him for the past five minutes. She spoke loudly and clearly, obviously accustomed to topping the ferocious roar of machinery.

"Oh, so your father and Henri have been friends for years?"

"Yes, that's right."

"And where did you say you're from?"

"I didn't say, but we live quite close to Lyon."

"How do they know each other then? Lyon's a long way away."

"They were friends in the army, and they've stayed in contact ever since."

"Oh, that's nice. It's good to have old friends; we all need friends. And how long will you be staying, Paul?"

"Sorry?" Paul said, the looms thundering in his ears. He leaned closer. "I didn't hear what you said."

"How long will you be staying with us?" Yvette mouthed slowly and deliberately.

"I don't know," Paul answered with a shake of his head. "My dad wants me to learn all about the business, to see if I want to make a career in it. So Henri said I should work everywhere in the factory, starting with Didier's area."

Yvette nodded slowly. "Yes, Didier's a good lad; he'll start you off in the right direction. But you make sure that when it's time to learn about operating a loom you come to me, all right?"

"I will."

"Don't forget now; you tell them you want Yvette to teach you the loom."

"Yes, I will. Thank you."

Yvette grinned and pinched Paul's cheek. "What a nice polite young man. It'll be a pleasure having you here, Paul."

Paul smiled and strolled back to Didier's workshop. He was still smiling as he went inside and closed the door.

"Well?" Didier asked.

"It was exactly as you and Henri said. Yvette cornered me the moment she saw I was alone. Then she asked me every question you'd thought of, and a few more."

"Anything that had you worried?"

Paul thought for a moment and then shook his head. "No, it was all pretty harmless, I think."

"Good. As Henri always says, one conversation with Yvette Bigou is better than a whole-page story in the local newspaper. Everyone in the factory and half the town will know all about you by this evening. At least, they'll know what we want them to know, and that's better than dangerous wild guesses."

Or not so wild, Paul thought to himself, imagining the trek across the mountains to Spain he was soon to make.

"We can't be too careful," Didier went on, "and we don't want any rumours circulating. We don't know who betrayed Jean-Pierre, but whoever he is, he's still out there."

"Perhaps it's a woman," Paul answered, suddenly reminded of a conversation from earlier in his journey. Back on the *Marina* he and Albert had wondered about the identity of the traitor in Antwerp; now here in Lavelanet, he and Didier were doing the same thing. In both north and south it appeared that treachery was never far away.

"Come on, there's work to be done," Didier said,

breaking in on Paul's thoughts. He pointed to a large metal drum on one side of the workshop. "That's grease and next to it is a bucket full of nuts and bolts that need greasing. It's about time you got your hands dirty. And those new overalls too."

Paul set about his task, working steadily, the thick grease coating his fingers. He felt a bit like a kid playing in the mud and realized that he hadn't felt like a kid for a long time.

"I've been wanting to apologize to you," he said, looking over at Didier.

"For what?"

"For being so ignorant about General de Gaulle, and the battles, and the Free French Forces in England. I should have known."

Didier shrugged. "I guess you didn't hear his broadcast on the BBC radio, the appeal of the eighteenth of June?"

Paul shook his head.

"It was the most stirring speech I've ever heard," Didier said. "He appealed to all true French patriots, and told us to resist the Nazis and continue the struggle." He fell silent, lost in thoughts of his own. Then he smiled. "One day he will be back, leading the Free French Forces. I'm certain we'll see him in France again."

"And is he the reason you've joined with Henri and the others?"

"He's not the reason," Didier said. "Just the inspiration."

Paul slowly screwed a freshly greased nut onto a bolt before answering. "There's so much I didn't think about until little more than a week ago," he said, tossing the nut and bolt into the bucket. "But I do now, and I'd like to help."

"So how is the young gentleman from the north getting on?" Josette asked Didier. "I bet he wasn't very happy at getting dirt under his fingernails."

"To be fair, he's doing all right," Didier replied. "And he's not so bad, once you get to know him."

"After the past few days I know enough," Josette said, frown lines creasing her forehead. "He thinks he's better than the rest of us."

"No, you're wrong there. This is all very different for him; it takes time to adjust. Give him a chance."

Josette didn't reply.

"Anyway," Didier said, "I'm taking him for a ride on the bike later on. I thought I'd show him some of the countryside."

Work was over for the day and they were sitting on a low wall close to the factory, catching the late-afternoon sun. Josette tilted her head back so that its rays could warm her cheeks. "He didn't even wait to walk home with me."

"Did you ask him to wait?"

"Why should I ask him?" Josette said, frowning again.

Didier laughed. "As far as I know he's not a mind-reader.

And, anyway, by not walking home with him you have the pleasure of my company for a little longer."

Josette couldn't stop herself from laughing as she turned to look at Didier. "And what makes you think I enjoy your company?"

"It's obvious," Didier said with a shrug. He glanced around. There was no one nearby but he lowered his voice when he spoke. "Paul's had a tough time, Josette."

"Yes, I know about his father," Josette said, "it's awful."

"It's not just his father; his mother was taken away by the Germans too. And then…" Didier took another look around and moved closer to Josette. Speaking in little more than a whisper he told her about the fight with the man on the train. "It's the truth," he said. "Paul fought for his life and defeated an enemy of France. That's a lot more than you or I have done in this war, so at the very least he deserves our respect."

TWENTY-SIX

Paul soon settled into his new role at the factory. Over the next few days he proved himself capable at basic mechanical jobs, impressing Didier with his effort and attitude.

"Keep your head down and get on with the job," was Henri's advice on day one and Paul was doing exactly as instructed.

The factory foreman, Marcel Castelnaud, was slightly put out at not being informed earlier about the new member of the workforce, but a few soothing words from Henri quickly restored his usual good humour. As for the rest of the staff, their initial interest soon waned, to be replaced by a friendly indifference towards Paul. With one exception, Yvette Bigou.

Ever-inquisitive Yvette seemed to want to take the new boy under her wing. And she had an uncanny knack of homing in on him whenever he was alone on the factory floor.

Then the grilling would begin.

"So, you're living with Henri and Hélène?"

"Yes, at the moment."

"Such nice people, and good friends of mine. Will you be staying on here, then?"

"I don't know, we'll have to see."

"Oh, I do hope so. It's so nice to have a handsome new face in the factory."

She was relentless, and Paul had to be inventive with excuses to make his escape. "I'd better get back to Didier, he needs me to hold the ladder."

"Which ladder?"

"See you later, Yvette."

Paul was always eager to escape Yvette's clutches, but Josette was a different matter. She came looking for him the day after her conversation with Didier and got straight to the point. "I'm sorry for the things I said when we went for that walk."

"It's all right," Paul replied, slightly surprised. "I shouldn't have said what I said about the accent. And I didn't mean—"

"I know," Josette said, interrupting. She hesitated and then smiled shyly. "We got off to a bad start, didn't we?"

Paul was momentarily lost for words. This was a new side to Josette. She was softer, friendlier and her dark brown eyes were warm and sincere rather than fiery and hostile. As Paul stared, he realized that her eyes were actually very beautiful.

"Yes, we did," he managed to say.

"Maybe we could start again?"

Paul nodded. "I'd like that."

"And I won't ask you so many questions."

"You can ask me questions." He smiled. "I might not answer them, but you can ask."

Over the next couple of days Josette did ask further questions, and so did Paul. Not about the war or dangerous secrets but about themselves; their likes and dislikes, their dreams and ambitions. Almost without realizing it they discovered that they wanted to know about each other because they liked each other. Liked each other a lot.

The following Saturday morning, Josette suggested they take another walk into the town. "I promise it won't be like the last time," she told him.

It was a fine, bright day. They looked in a few shop windows, Paul bought himself the sturdy pair of walking boots he would soon need and afterwards Josette suggested they stop for a drink on a café terrace.

"Good idea," Paul said. They had passed a café on the main street and he turned to retrace his steps.

"No, not that café," Josette said quickly. "I know a better one."

She strode quickly away and Paul had no option but to follow. Turning off the main street they arrived at a small, tree-lined square.

"That's the place," Josette said.

She led the way onto the café terrace and took a seat at a table beneath the awning, close to the wide front window.

"We're in the shade here," Paul said. "Wouldn't you rather be in the sun?"

"No, this is fine," Josette said quickly. "If you don't mind."

Paul shrugged. Remembering Josette's explosive temper he sat down without comment.

A man emerged from inside the café. "Ah, Josette," he said, smiling. "And how are you?"

"Very well, Victor, thank you," Josette replied.

Victor nodded at Paul and then looked at Josette, waiting for an introduction. It didn't come. Josette simply ordered their drinks and said nothing more.

"He probably knows who you are anyway," she said to Paul once Victor had gone. "Everyone knows everyone in Lavelanet."

Their soft drinks arrived quickly. They were alone on the terrace and just a few customers were sitting inside the café.

"So, what's so special about this place?" Paul asked. "It's not very busy."

"This is where Jean-Pierre Dilhat came to talk," Josette answered in a hushed voice.

"To talk?"

"To try to get others to join the … you know, the fight."

"But that doesn't tell me why we're here," Paul said.

Josette stole a quick look through the window to the dark

interior. "My dad, Didier and Gaston are all concentrating on getting you over the mountains. But there's a traitor in Lavelanet, the person who betrayed Jean-Pierre. And when you're in Spain and on your way to England the traitor will still be here. So we have to find him."

"We?"

"I," Josette said. "But I'd like your help."

"I'll be gone in a few days."

"Perhaps we'll only need a few days. Lavelanet is a small place, and like I said, everyone…"

"…knows everyone," Paul said.

"Exactly."

Paul thought for a moment and then nodded. "Tell me what you know."

Josette smiled. "I'm not certain of anything, of course, but maybe the people here weren't as trustworthy as Jean-Pierre believed."

"Here? You mean at this café?"

Josette nodded. "There's Victor Forêt, for a start."

"The man who brought our drinks?"

Josette nodded again. "He owns the café, but every time I was here I could see he didn't agree with Jean-Pierre. It was obvious, and he always argued against taking action."

"That doesn't make him a traitor."

"I know, but…" Josette fell silent before gesturing with her head towards the window. "You see those two young men sitting at the bar? Don't let them see you looking."

Paul picked up his drink, took a sip and at the same time glanced through the window at the two men. "What about them?"

"Alain Noury and Yves Besson. They work at the comb factory, but from what I see they're always here. They let Jean-Pierre buy them drinks, but they didn't join him in the fight."

Paul snatched another look at the two men. "Maybe they realized that if they listened to what he said they'd get another free drink."

Josette's eyes flashed. "Are you laughing at me?"

"No, I'm not, honestly, Josette," Paul said. "But we need a lot more to go on than what you've told me. A few words from the café owner and few free drinks for the other two – it's not evidence, is it?"

"No," Josette agreed with a sigh.

"Is there anyone else you suspect?" Paul asked. "Not necessarily someone at this café?"

Josette sighed. "I made a terrible mistake over Papa and Gaston Rouzard."

"Yes, I know."

"But there's another gendarme officer, Bertrand Picou. I've never liked him; he can be a really nasty piece of work."

"But that doesn't make him a traitor either. And, anyway, your father said Jean-Pierre was arrested by officers from … where was it? Another town near here…"

"Mirepoix. Bertrand Picou could have tipped them off."

"You're just guessing. Or picking on people you don't like."

Josette stared stubbornly at Paul and then sank back in her chair with a sigh of frustration. "I was hoping you'd see something I've missed."

"You probably haven't missed anything," Paul said. "But you probably haven't found the right person."

They finished their drinks, each deep in thought, and neither heard footsteps approaching on the pavement.

"Hello, you two. What's this, a secret romantic rendezvous?"

Gaston Rouzard was standing at the edge of the terrace, smiling broadly.

"Don't be silly, Gaston," Josette said hurriedly, blushing. "We just stopped for a drink. It's hot."

Gaston winked and tapped the side of his nose with an index finger. "Yes, and I'll be certain not to mention to young Didier that I saw you."

He laughed and then continued on his way.

Paul and Josette sat in embarrassed silence, both staring at their empty glasses.

"I … I, er, didn't know," Paul said eventually.

"Know what?"

"About Didier."

"What about Didier?"

"You and… Is he your boyfriend?"

"No, he is not my boyfriend," Josette snapped. "Didier is my friend. Probably my best friend, but that's all."

"Oh. Right."

"And for your information, I'm not interested in boy-friends. I told Didier and now I'm telling you." She got to her feet. "Understood?"

Paul nodded. "Understood."

TWENTY-SEVEN

"**E**verything is arranged; we're ready to move."

Paul glanced quickly at Josette and then back at Henri. "When?"

"Tomorrow night."

Paul's eyes widened. "That soon?"

"It must be tomorrow," Henri said. "We free Jean-Pierre Dilhat from the camp at midnight. You'll be at a safe house here in Lavelanet and when we return from Rivel we'll take you both to the team waiting to lead you over the mountains."

They all stared at Paul – Henri, Gaston, Didier, Hélène and Josette – waiting for his response. The final phase of the operation was to commence in little more than twenty-four hours, but for a few seconds he didn't know what to say.

"How will you get Jean-Pierre out?" he asked eventually.

Henri glanced at Gaston, who nodded. "We've bribed one of the guards," Gaston said. "I'll see him tomorrow to give him his first payment. He gets the rest when you and Jean-Pierre are safely in Spain."

Paul's mind was racing. For some reason, which he couldn't quite grasp, he didn't feel elated by the news. He felt confused, but there was no time to work out why.

"There's more you need to know, Paul," Henri said. "Jean-Pierre has just been released from solitary confinement. And he's in poor shape, according to Gaston's contact."

"It's his own fault," Gaston snapped angrily. "He should have kept his mouth shut, but instead he got himself punished for insubordination and inciting the other prisoners to protest. Bloody fool!"

Henri placed a hand on Gaston's arm. "There's nothing we can do about it now, my friend," he said softly. He turned to Paul. "It means that your journey across the mountains could be more difficult than we anticipated. You may need to help Jean-Pierre."

Josette had been biting her tongue, desperate to join in the conversation but certain that her father would not welcome her comments. But she couldn't stay silent any longer. "Wouldn't it be better to wait until Jean-Pierre has recovered and is stronger?"

"We can't wait," Henri said. "The mountain team is ready now and this will almost certainly be the last opportunity before the weather breaks. Once that happens a crossing is impossible."

"And it's not only the crossing," Gaston added gruffly. "They won't put up with troublemakers in the camp; another spell in solitary and Jean-Pierre…" he paused, his eyes going from Josette to Hélène, "…well, it might be more than he can take."

Hélène gasped, putting a hand to her mouth.

"Don't worry," Henri said quickly to his wife, "we'll get him out, I promise."

Despite his brave words the atmosphere in the room was suddenly thick with anxiety.

Paul looked at the three men seated opposite. They were ordinary men, not trained soldiers or highly skilled covert operators. They were stepping into unknown and uncertain territory, their first real taste of action. Organizing and coordinating his escape across the mountains was risky enough, and the planned freeing of Jean-Pierre Dilhat from the internment camp only added to the danger.

They were all heroes as far as Paul was concerned. "I'll do everything I can to help Jean-Pierre," he said to Henri. "I won't let you down."

Henri smiled. "I know that, Paul, thank you. Now, tomorrow we must all act as though nothing is different. At the factory, it's a normal working day – we must not arouse suspicions."

"And when work is over?" Hélène asked.

"We'll return here as usual, and before I leave for Rivel I'll take Paul to the safe house." He turned to Paul. "I'll be giving you a lot of money. Enough to pay your guides the remainder of their fee when you reach Spain and more to use as you need it, to make certain you and Jean-Pierre reach England safely."

"But how will we know they've got there safely?" Josette asked her father anxiously.

"We'll know," Henri replied. "A message will come through on the radio. And then we will celebrate, eh?"

He laughed, but it was forced and artificial. Henri looked pale and weary, and Paul could see that the strain of planning the operation and the responsibility it brought were beginning to tell.

Hélène had noticed it too. "You look tired, Henri."

"Me? No, I'm fine," Henri said with a smile and a shrug of his shoulders. "But now, Gaston, Didier and I must talk about Jean-Pierre and Rivel, so if you and Josette and Paul…"

"Of course," Hélène said.

Josette took a deep breath, about to demand that they be allowed to stay, but she saw Didier watching, silently suggesting she say nothing. He gave her a wink, and reluctantly she got to her feet and followed her mother from the room.

Paul was about to leave too, but Henri signalled for him to wait. "One more thing, Paul," he said, when he was certain Hélène and Josette were out of earshot. "There was a radio message broadcast last night. It seems that your friend in Antwerp has been released by the Germans."

"Jos Theys?"

"I think so. Although no one is using real names on the radio now, just code-names, so I can't be certain. But I believe it's him."

"So … so what does it mean?"

"It can only mean he managed to convince the Nazis he's not part of the Resistance movement. I thought you should know."

"Thank you," Paul said. "And there was nothing about my mother?"

"I'm afraid not."

Paul nodded and turned to leave, but at the open doorway he stopped and looked back. "Thank you," he said again, but this time it was to all three men sitting at the table.

He stepped from the room and pulled the heavy door shut. As he turned around, out of nowhere, there was Josette.

"Come with me," she whispered.

They were lying face down and side by side on the floor of Josette's bedroom, ears pressed to the floor.

"Something tells me you've done this before," Paul whispered.

"Shh," Josette breathed, "I want to hear what they're saying."

In the room below, Henri, Gaston and Didier were speaking quietly as they discussed the plan for freeing Jean-Pierre Dilhat from the camp at Rivel.

"So, tomorrow afternoon," Henri said, "Gaston takes the train to Chalabre to meet with his Rivel contact and confirms that he must have Jean-Pierre ready by the fence at midnight – away from the road, on the south side, where it's darkest."

"And I give him half the money," Gaston added. "He gets the rest later."

"But the other guards," Didier said, "I'm still worried about them."

"I told you before," Gaston said, "we don't need to worry. No one has escaped – or even tried to escape – from the camp. The guards hardly bother to check the huts and never patrol the fences at night. They'll sleep through the whole thing."

"Maybe it will change after tomorrow night," Didier said.

"After tomorrow night doesn't concern us," Gaston said irritably. "So can we move on, please?"

"All right," Henri said, "let's all keep calm, eh?" There was a moment of silence before he continued. "We take two vehicles to Rivel. Didier takes his motorcycle by the back roads, while Léon Anglade and I drive there in the truck, using the main road."

In the room above, Paul caught Josette's eye and mouthed almost silently, "Who is Léon Anglade?"

"From Foix," Josette whispered. "A friend of Papa's."

"Once we have freed Jean-Pierre," Henri continued, "Léon and I return to Lavelanet by the same route…"

"While I take Jean-Pierre to the safe house on the bike, using the back roads again," Didier said.

Paul was trying to figure out why this man named Léon Anglade had suddenly joined the operation. The answer came from Gaston Rouzard.

"I'm sorry I can't be with you," he said, "but it's too risky. An off-duty trip to see an old colleague in Chalabre is easy enough to explain. But these days, even when I'm off duty the station has to know where I am. The new regulations tell us it's in case of an emergency." He laughed. "When did we last have an emergency in Lavelanet?"

"Of course," Henri told him, "everything must be as normal as possible here. Léon is a good man and completely trustworthy. And we'll need him later anyway, as he knows the contact who knows the mountain team – and I don't."

Paul smiled as he heard Henri's words, recognizing that the "need to know" rule was maintained as strictly in the south as in the north.

Down below, Didier was still worrying about the internment camp guards. "*If* the escape is discovered and the alarm goes off, the truck will almost certainly be stopped by the gendarmes."

"How many times must I tell you," Gaston barked, "the escape won't be discovered until the morning at the earliest."

"No, Didier's right," Henri said quietly, playing the peacemaker again. "We must consider every possibility.

And it is possible the escape will be discovered and the truck stopped. And that would mean trouble if you, a gendarme officer, were to be found with me. But Léon is in the textile business too, so it's not unlikely we'd be moving material together, even late at night. It makes it much safer for us all."

"And what if you are stopped?" Didier asked. "We haven't discussed that."

Josette and Paul heard Henri give a chuckle. "I almost hope we are, as ours is the diversionary tactic. Tomorrow I'll make sure the truck is heavily, and badly, loaded. If we're stopped it will take the gendarmes an age to search all the way through it. Time enough for you to get safely back to Lavelanet, Didier."

Aware that his ear had gone numb, Paul turned and pressed his other ear to the floor.

"Then Léon and I take Jean-Pierre and Paul to the rendezvous with the mountain team," Paul heard Henri say. "Léon knows the place."

"And which trail will they take?" Didier asked. "Do we know yet?"

"Yes," Henri said softly. "It's the Eagle Trail."

TWENTY-EIGHT

Josette suddenly realized she was grasping Paul's hand. She had closed her eyes, concentrating fully on what was being said in the room below. Opening them she saw Paul staring at her. His face was close to hers. He smiled and squeezed her fingers, and she instantly released her grip and looked away, her cheeks burning.

She had never heard of the Eagle Trail, but the name was enough to send a shiver down her spine. It sounded dark and brooding, menacing and deadly dangerous. It made her heart thud. It made her grab Paul's hand again for comfort.

She blushed once more and pressed her face to the floor, trying to hide her embarrassment.

"I know the Eagle Trail," she heard Didier say in the room below.

"What do you mean?" Gaston snapped.

"Not the whole trail, but the beginning part. The first few hours are easy; the path is well trodden and clearly marked. But then it disappears completely; no signs, no markers, nothing at all. It's called the Eagle Trail because they say you need the eyes of an eagle to follow it."

"Yes, and because there are always eagles up above it," Gaston said. "We all know that, but how do you know the trail?"

Didier hesitated before replying. "My father died there."

Josette froze.

"I went on my bike once," Didier continued. "I wanted to see for myself where it happened. I walked for hours but when the trail petered out I had to turn back. It's easy to get lost up there." He turned to Henri. "I'll come with you tomorrow night."

"No, that will only complicate matters," Gaston said, before Henri could reply. "We've made our plan. Henri will have Léon with him; all they have to do is hand over Jean-Pierre and the boy to the mountain team. What could be simpler?"

"I'm just trying to help," Didier said.

"But you're not," Gaston said, his voice growing louder again. "When you get Jean-Pierre back from Rivel you'll have done your bit, so leave it at that."

"But I'm worried about Jean-Pierre – and Paul, come to that!"

"Look, just stick to the plan, Didier, and don't—"

"Enough!" Henri said loudly. "Stop it, both of you!"

There was a tense silence and then Henri spoke again, quietly. "There's no point in arguing among ourselves, it won't help anyone. Perhaps it would be useful to have you with us tomorrow, Didier. I'll think it through and—"

"But it's complicating the operation," Gaston said, interrupting. "And if we compli—" He fell silent under Henri's penetrating stare.

Henri waited for a moment, then picked up where he had left off. "So I'll think it through, Didier, and let you know tomorrow what I've decided."

Gaston sighed loudly and irritably, making it clear that he disagreed.

"Stay calm, my friend," Henri said to him kindly. "We're all a little tense, I know. But we need to stay positive, for Paul especially. Because if Jean-Pierre is in as bad a shape as we fear, then a lot will depend on him."

Josette turned her head and held Paul's gaze.

The tension and uncertainty below seemed to seep up through the floorboards to wrap them both in an icy grip.

TWENTY-NINE

The day was passing with agonizing slowness. Henri, Josette, Paul and Didier were attempting to work normally – and failing dismally. The events of the night to come and the threat of the unknown hung heavily in the air.

Josette stayed mainly in the office, starting one small job after another and completing none. Her mind was in turmoil. She was afraid for her father, for Didier and for Paul, collectively and individually. And she was tormented by the knowledge that if the plan went wrong she would be powerless to intervene.

Henri took his time supervising the loading of the truck before joining Josette in the office. A few minutes later he leapt to his feet and hurried back out to make certain he had packed strong wire-cutters and torches in the driver's cab. He had. He trudged back up the stairs to the office but ran down again a few minutes later to make absolutely sure the truck's fuel tank was full. It was.

When he was finally settled at his desk he simply sat

gazing into space. After a while Josette glanced up from her own desk. Her father looked exhausted. There were dark rings beneath his eyes and his skin had a grey, ghostly pallor. He had obviously hardly slept, though Josette had fared little better.

The next time she looked up at her father, he was smoothing the bristles of his moustache. On any other day Josette would have simply shrugged and smiled, but not today. Today the familiar sight was suddenly infuriating.

"Papa!" she almost yelled.

Henri looked over from his desk. "Yes? What is it?"

"The moustache! Please will you stop doing that!"

"Oh! Sorry! I didn't realize."

"It drives me mad, Papa."

"Really? You should have mentioned it before."

Josette rolled her eyes, took a deep breath and went back to the accounts ledger she'd been working on for what felt like a lifetime. When she looked up a few minutes later Henri was staring into space, rhythmically smoothing down his moustache once again.

Paul was in the workshop, listlessly moving tools from one bench to another. Unable to suggest anything more useful, Didier had told him to tidy up. However Didier prided himself on keeping a perfectly tidy workshop, so there was little for Paul to do.

Paul also had much on his mind. Firstly there was the news from Antwerp that Jos Theys had been freed. He was finding it difficult to understand. His father had been gunned down, his mother had been arrested and was still in captivity – or worse – but Jos had been allowed to go free.

There could be only one explanation. Jos must have perfected a totally convincing cover story, one good enough to satisfy even his Nazi interrogators. That had to be it. Paul trusted Jos. Jos had started him on his flight to safety. But at the back of Paul's mind there was also a nagging doubt. Could Jos have betrayed his father? No – he pushed that awful thought away too.

Paul was also thinking about Josette.

The previous evening when the meeting in the room below had broken up, he and Josette had scrambled to their feet as quietly as possible. Paul had mumbled a quick, "Goodnight," and then hurried off to his own room without waiting for a response.

Since then they had not been alone together. This morning, Josette had missed breakfast, and when they walked to the factory with Henri, neither had said a word.

But as Paul lifted a spanner from the bench and then put it down in exactly the same position, he found himself puzzling over his feelings towards her and wondering about her feelings for him.

To complicate things further, there was Didier. Paul knew that Didier was crazy about Josette. Everyone knew it. And Didier had been looking out for Paul since he'd first set foot in the factory. They'd become friends; the last thing

Paul wanted to do was to hurt a friend.

Paul sighed, deciding that in reality none of this confusion over Josette and Didier mattered anyway. By the same time tomorrow he would be high in the mountains, somewhere on the Eagle Trail, forced to focus on nothing but his and Jean-Pierre's long climb to freedom. Once that climb began he was unlikely to see Josette or Didier, or Lavelanet, ever again.

The thought did not make him feel better.

Didier was probably the most conscientious worker in the entire factory, but even he was struggling to stop his thoughts being drawn to the night ahead.

He spent the morning aimlessly tinkering with a machine that had been out of action for months. At lunchtime he checked and rechecked every moving part of his motorbike, adjusted the tyre pressures and made sure the fuel tank was topped up. Then he rode the bike to Henri's house, leaving it there in readiness for his late-night journey to Rivel.

He walked back to the factory deep in thought, and as he passed through the main doors came face to face with Josette.

They stared at each other.

"Hello," Didier said.

Josette didn't answer, but he noticed the tears in her eyes. She rushed up the staircase without a word.

"Josette?" he called.

Gloomily, Didier trudged back to the workshop, nodding a greeting to Paul and sat down at his bench. He picked up a clipboard and glanced idly at the job sheet fixed to it, without taking in any of the words.

"Have you spoken to Josette?" he asked eventually.

"Not since this morning."

"Was she all right?"

"I ... I think so."

"I saw her when I came in. She seemed upset."

Paul said nothing and they lapsed into an uneasy silence.

"Probably just worried," Didier said a couple of minutes later. "About tonight."

"Yes," Paul answered unconvincingly, "that's probably it."

They fell silent again, both wanting to talk but equally unsure what to talk about.

"I ... I..."

"Yes?" Didier said.

"I wanted to ask you about the mountains."

"What about them?"

Paul knew he couldn't ask Didier directly about the Eagle Trail. He wasn't meant to know about it. "No one has told me much," he said. "I don't know what to expect; I'd like some idea before we start."

Didier thought before answering. "Yes, you should know at least something. Well, it won't be easy, I can tell you that."

"And can you tell me any more?"

"People have always crossed the Pyrenees," Didier continued. "Until a year or so ago many were coming from Spain into France to escape the civil war there. Now they go in the opposite direction to escape our war. The camp at Rivel was originally built to house refugees from Spain." He shook his head sadly. "There are more like it all along the border. Our government didn't even need to build new ones."

"And are there many routes across the mountains?"

"A few," Didier said, "some much more dangerous than others. But the most dangerous to cross are also the safest to use."

Paul frowned. "I don't understand."

"Few people even attempt them," Didier said, "so the chances of being caught by border guards are very slim. Some of them have names. The Wolf Trail, because it's said that wolves used to hunt there. And the Lion Trail."

"Lion?" Paul said. "I didn't know there were lions in the Pyrenees!"

"It's because there's a huge rock high up that's shaped like a lion's head. And then there's the Eagle Trail."

He paused.

"What about the Eagle Trail?" Paul asked.

"It's probably the most dangerous of all. My father loved the mountains. He knew them well, but he lost his footing and died on the Eagle Trail." Didier looked at Paul. "We both lost our fathers too soon. Something else we have in common, eh?"

"Something else?" Paul said. "You've confused me again."

Didier smiled. "Well, we're both mad about Josette, aren't we?"

Paul stared. Until that moment he'd had no idea that his feelings for Josette were apparent to anyone else. He wasn't even sure how he felt about her himself. He was struggling to answer when there was a knock at the door and the ever-smiling Marcel Castelnaud came in and asked Didier if he would take a look at a machine that had mysteriously stopped working.

Didier picked up his tool bag. "I'll catch you up," he said to Marcel, and the factory foreman sauntered away.

Didier crossed to the doorway, checked that no one was nearby and turned back to Paul. "I'm sorry if I've been a bit miserable today."

"You haven't," Paul said. "At least, no more miserable than me."

"We're all a bit tense, I guess."

"It's the waiting."

Didier nodded. "Well, it won't be long now."

He disappeared, leaving Paul deep in thought. Paul glanced at the neat line of tools he had rearranged on the bench earlier in the day. He sighed, and because he had nothing else to do, began shifting them round again, back to their original position.

A few minutes later, a piercing scream cut through the constant thundering of the machines. Paul sprang to his feet. There was another scream and then another, and then an emergency siren began to wail. Paul hurtled to the doorway just as Yvette Bigou ran past, rushing towards the stairs to the office, her face white and streaked with tears.

"Yvette!" Paul shouted. "Yvette, what's happened?"

Yvette came to a standstill, her eyes wide with horror. "It's Didier! He fell into the machine. There's blood – everywhere. I think … I think he's dead!"

THIRTY

Gaston Rouzard sat back on the less-than-comfortable, sparely padded bench and glanced through the carriage window at the countryside he loved.

The single-track Moulin-Neuf rail link ran from Lavelanet to Mirepoix and was the simplest way to reach the small town of Chalabre, particularly for someone like Gaston, who had never learned to drive a car.

The Moulin-Neuf was a special rail line, Gaston believed, as not only did it link the industrial Hers valley, named after the river that meandered through it, with the national rail network, it also brought within easy reach the cluster of villages he had known throughout his life. There were small stations at Laroque-d'Olmes, La Bastide-sur-l'Hers, Le Peyrat and Sainte-Colombe-sur-l'Hers, before the train reached the bigger station at Chalabre.

The day was overcast, with low clouds moving briskly in a sharp breeze, but for Gaston, the short journey was always delightful and restful, and one he had made many times.

He had never wanted to travel far; Lavelanet and the Hers valley was his stomping ground. Even during the First World War, when other young men of the area were fighting at the front, Gaston's job as a gendarme officer meant he could remain behind to keep order on the home front.

And order was what he liked. Order in everything.

As the train moved sedately through the countryside, Gaston smiled at each familiar landmark; the unusual church tower at Le Peyrat, with its row of three bells hanging near the top and a fourth bell suspended alone just below, was a particular favourite.

Leaving the village, the train entered the long, straight section of track leading to the station at Sainte-Colombe-sur-l'Hers. Gaston stared out at the high, tree-blanketed hills to his right. His favourite time of the year was fast approaching – the hunting season. Soon he would be out in those hills, prowling the woods with his trusty shotgun broken over one arm, accompanied by his shooting friends and a pack of baying hounds. Wild fowl and deer were fun – good sport and excellent practice. But his favourite prey – the only prey that really mattered – was the wild boar, the *sanglier*.

Gaston loved tracking, stalking, pursuing and finally running down the mighty *sanglier*. He loved the thrill of the chase, but most of all he loved the moment of execution, staring down the barrel of his shotgun and pulling the trigger as the brave animal charged to its death.

The *sanglier* was a noble beast, cautious but courageous, a tranquil, even gentle animal when left to get on with its life in peace. But it was also a ferocious opponent, prepared to fight to the death when threatened or cornered. A lot like Gaston himself.

Gaston had chosen "Sanglier" as his code-name. He hadn't used the name yet, or even told anyone about it. But when he was ready, when he took over, he would send out his own coded radio messages, carefully broadcasting mis-information to all those who sought to change things and destroy the tranquillity of his life. They were the real trai-tors of France, and they would be dealt with, Henri first and foremost.

The fact that Henri did not hunt, did not shoot for pleas-ure, was just one of the reasons why Gaston despised his so-called friend.

They had been at school together, but it was only fairly recently, when Henri announced that he would lead the local Resistance movement, that Gaston came to realize that he had probably always hated Henri.

As a boy, he had envied the fact that Henri would one day inherit the family business and never have to struggle for money, as Gaston and his family had. Even when Gaston became a gendarme officer, he had to support his elderly parents in the long years before they died. Since then, he had got by; a gendarme's pay would never make him rich. He didn't need to be rich, just better off, and his new venture would certainly improve his financial situation.

The train stopped at Sainte-Colombe-sur-l'Hers station, which sat on the edge of the village. No one got into Gaston's compartment, and he was pleased to remain alone with his thoughts and his plans.

The whistle sounded and the train moved on. Gaston checked his wristwatch, noting with satisfaction that Didier would by now have been dispatched. He was a trouble-maker; too keen, too questioning, too interfering – and wanting to be involved in the last part of tonight's operation had been the final straw. Gaston didn't want to risk further complications, so he had acted – swiftly and decisively. It would have happened soon enough anyway.

The others would be similarly dealt with in due course, even Henri's brattish daughter, Josette, who had almost ruined everything with her stupid guesses and hasty accusations.

Gaston was convinced that, despite the setback with Didier, Henri would continue with tonight's operation. He had to; there was no alternative. With Didier out of the picture, the plan would have to be amended a little, but that was nothing Gaston need worry about.

He smiled to himself. Too many people had been under-estimating him for too long. They'd all come to realize that when he took over.

As the train passed sedately along the embankment at the top of the village, Gaston looked out at the red-tiled rooftops and glimpsed a handful of villagers going about their day-to-day business. He was certain that they, like him and thousands of others, wanted nothing to do with the war or with the occupation of northern France. They wanted stability and order. Marshal Pétain and the Vichy government would ensure both.

And so would he, Sanglier, with the help of true friends and patriots, those who felt the same way he did. He had already begun to recruit and once he was fully in charge, more would join. He was certain of that too.

The train gathered speed as the track curved a little downhill. Soon it was passing close to the village of Rivel.

A temporary station had recently been constructed near to the internment camp. Few trains had stopped there so far but before long they would stop frequently, as the current batch of prisoners were taken away to north Africa and others brought in to await transportation to different destinations.

Troublemakers, all of them, Gaston thought to himself, as he glimpsed the wire fence and, beyond it, the brown-suited prisoners in the compound.

The next stop was Chalabre. The train slowed and Gaston got to his feet, feeling his inside pocket to check that the envelope containing the wad of notes Henri had given him was safely in place. He dusted down his uniform and lowered the window in the carriage door.

With a shudder and a squeal of brakes the train halted.

Gaston reached through the open window to push down the handle. He opened the door and stepped onto the platform, instantly spotting his old friend and colleague, Raymond Martel, who raised a hand in greeting.

"Ah, Raymond," Gaston said as they shook hands, "it's good to see you again. You have a busy night ahead of you."

THIRTY-ONE

It seemed impossible to Henri Mazet that Didier had fallen into the loading machine by accident. Didier was simply too careful, too aware that the machines he worked with daily were potential death traps, to be treated with the utmost care. *He didn't fall*, thought Henri, staring at the bloodstained mechanism. *He was pushed.*

The factory floor was deserted apart from Henri, who had sent everyone home. He was trying to figure out the sequence of events. The loading machine was used to raise heavy bundles of material to a conveyor belt, which ran high across the factory, close to the ceiling. Didier had pitched headlong into the lifting mechanism and become trapped in the drive belt. He must have twisted sideways at the last moment, as his left arm and shoulder and the left side of his head had taken the impact.

When they finally managed to free him, the full extent of his injuries was revealed. A long jagged gash, oozing blood, ran down the left side of his head, and there were further bloody wounds to his shoulder and arm. But he was alive. Unconscious and deathly pale, but breathing.

Henri had acted swiftly. He staunched the blood flow with clean bandages while barking out a string of orders to the petrified onlookers.

A doctor arrived within ten minutes and Didier was rushed to the local hospital. Paul went with him, while Josette was sent to fetch Didier's mother.

All the machines in the factory were shut down, but before dismissing the staff for the remainder of the day, Henri questioned everyone who had been in the vicinity of the accident. Or, as Henri now believed, the *incident*.

No one had seen a thing; at least, that's what they were saying.

An ashen-faced Marcel Castelnaud, unsmiling for once, said he'd simply fetched Didier to the machine after being told it had stopped working.

"And who told you?" Henri asked him.

"Joseph. He'd been using it in the morning and switched it off at lunchtime. He was on some other job in the early afternoon, but when he came back to the loader it wouldn't start. So he told me and I fetched Didier."

"And left him to it?"

"That's not unusual. I wouldn't normally stand and watch him do a repair. I was busy; I had other things to do."

Joseph confirmed everything the foreman said and added nothing to help solve the mystery.

Henri questioned others, including a tearful Yvette Bigou, first on the scene and still badly shaken.

"I was on the way back to my loom," she told Henri. "The loading machine had already shut down when I got there, but I think I heard Didier yell before I came around the corner. I'm not sure; you know how noisy it is. But then I saw Didier, trapped like that, and the blood…" She began to cry again. "That poor boy … and his poor mother…"

"Yes, Yvette, we must hope for the best." Henri answered gently. "And you saw no one else?"

"No one. No one at all," Yvette sobbed.

Henri received the same answer from everyone he questioned.

"No one at all," he repeated to himself, stepping back from the machine to get a wider view. He sighed. Whoever pushed Didier had picked the perfect spot to attempt a murder.

The loading machine was in an isolated position, hidden from the main part of the factory floor. Bundles of material to be shifted were brought up on trolleys. Several of these stood close by, further masking the machine from general view.

So, Henri decided, it was probably true that no one had witnessed the pushing.

Henri tried a different line of thought. Who, in the factory, might possibly want to harm Didier? More than hurt him, kill him?

"No one at all," Henri said again. Didier was one of the most popular members of the workforce. He had no enemies – not that Henri knew of. So it couldn't have been a personal grudge. There was only one possible explanation, the incident had to be connected with tonight's operation. Could there be a traitor in the team? The thought was painful but had to be considered.

A few people knew the full details of the operation: Henri himself, Didier, Léon Anglade and Gaston Rouzard. Neither Léon nor Gaston could have pushed Didier into the machine. They were nowhere near the factory when the incident happened. Léon was in Foix and Gaston was on a train travelling to Chalabre.

It had to be someone else, someone close by. But who? And why? Had someone let a vital piece of information slip? And was the person who tried to kill Didier also the one who betrayed Jean-Pierre Dilhat?

Henri was wracking his brains for answers when he heard footsteps approach. He turned around to see Josette and Paul. "How is he?"

Josette shook her head, unable to speak.

Paul answered for her. "Still unconscious. His mother's with him now so we thought it best to come back."

"And the doctors? What did they tell you?"

"Nothing very much. They did say that until he regains consciousness it's hard to tell if there's any permanent…"

Paul didn't continue, but Henri knew exactly what he meant.

"But they also said it looks as though there are no broken

bones," Josette said, finding her voice. "That's a good sign, isn't it, Papa?"

Henri smiled. "A very good sign, Josette. Very good indeed."

They fell silent, their eyes hypnotically drawn to the congealed blood on the machine. Henri was about to share his thoughts when he noticed how pale Josette looked. He decided to say nothing. It could wait; Josette and Paul had enough to worry about for now.

He nodded towards the machine. "I'll clean it up before we leave."

"No, let me," Paul said. "I'll get some water."

"Paul, wait a moment," Henri said before he had the chance to hurry away. "You must both be wondering, so I'll tell you now: tonight goes ahead as planned."

"But, Papa, you can't!" Josette said quickly. "It's too dangerous."

"Hardly more dangerous than before," her father said.

"But it is! There's no one to bring Jean-Pierre back to Lavelanet on the motorbike."

Henri was about to answer but then stopped. He spotted the guilty looks passing between Josette and Paul. "How do you two know about the motorcycle?"

Josette looked down at the floor and said nothing, so Henri turned to Paul, raising his eyebrows.

"We … we overheard you talking," Paul said. "To Didier and Gaston."

"You over—?" Henri hesitated and then spoke more urgently. "Did either of you mention any of what you heard to anyone – anyone at all?"

"No!" Paul and Josette said together.

"You're certain?"

"Yes!"

"Very well. Then it can't have had a bearing on what happened today." Frown lines crossed Henri's forehead and he glared sternly at his daughter. "Although I would like to know how you managed to overhear us through a locked door."

Josette still said nothing, and this time Paul stayed silent too.

"Perhaps you'll let me know in due course, eh, Josette?" Henri said.

"Perhaps," Josette said, in little more than a whisper. "But, Papa, it does mean that you can't go tonight."

"It means nothing of the sort. Léon and I…" He paused. "I suppose you know that Léon and I will be going to Rivel in one of the trucks?"

They both nodded.

"Yes, I thought so. Well then, Léon and I will bring Jean-Pierre back in the truck."

"But that's too dangerous!" Paul said. "You said yourself that the truck is the diversionary tactic."

Henri gave Paul a stern look. "Did you hear overhear absolutely everything that was discussed?"

"Just about."

"Then you'll know," Henri said abruptly, "that because the weather will undoubtedly change for the worse any day now, we have no choice but to go tonight."

"Actually you mentioned that before we left the room," Josette said, and then wished she hadn't as her father glared at her.

"Did I indeed? Thank you for reminding me, Josette." He sighed. "Anyway, the important fact is that as neither Léon nor I have ever ridden a motorbike, it has to be the truck."

"No!" Paul said, quickly. "It doesn't have to be the truck. I can ride the motorbike. I can bring Jean-Pierre back to Lavelanet."

"You?"

"I had a motorbike in Antwerp; I rode it every day, all over the city. I've been riding for over a year." He smiled confidently, well aware that he was deliberately holding back the full truth. The little machine on which he chugged around Antwerp was a completely different proposition to the powerful motorbike Didier rode.

"No, no, I couldn't possibly allow it," Henri said, shaking his head. "I couldn't possibly."

"But why not? I can do it, I know I can."

"But … but … you don't even know the way to Rivel."

"I do. Didier took me there on the bike the other evening, by the back roads. He didn't mention anything to me, but I see now that it must have been a trial run. I can remember the way, it's easy, just a couple of turns early on. After that it's almost straight."

"It's hardly straight, Paul. The back roads never stop twisting and turning."

"But it's only one road by then," Paul said again. "You just have to remind me where I need to make the turns."

Josette was staring at Paul, looking as though she didn't know whether to beg him not to be so stupid or to hug him for his bravery.

"Paul, I can't let you do this," Henri said again. "It's our job to get you safely across the mountains. That will be gruelling, so you must rest until we return from Rivel with Jean-Pierre."

"You know I won't be able to rest," Paul answered. "And you know the bike will be much safer than bringing Jean-Pierre back in the truck. If you're stopped with him, the whole operation is blown and neither of us will get across the mountains."

He could see that Henri was wavering. "Please, Henri," he went on quickly. "You've done so much for me, everyone has. This is my chance to do something in return, to repay you all, and Didier especially. Let me do it. For him."

THIRTY-TWO

It was ten o'clock, windy and dark, with low clouds blanketing the town. Motorbike and truck were about to depart, because although both journeys would take less than an hour, Henri wanted them all at Rivel well before the midnight rendezvous at the internment camp fence.

Both vehicles were parked at the front of the house, hidden from the road by a low wall, high railings and a thick hedge.

They were ready to go, but Henri wanted to see Paul safely away before he and Léon Anglade set off. He'd gone over Paul's route carefully, telling him exactly which turnings to take and where they were to meet at Rivel: a secluded hiding place just outside the village, but away from the camp.

Good news had come in a phone call to the hospital – Didier had regained consciousness. He was suffering concussion and was groggy and confused, with no recollection of his fall into the machine.

And there was a new worry; no word had come through from Gaston Rouzard. He should have returned from Chalabre long before now to confirm that his contact would be ready with Jean-Pierre at midnight. Henri had heard nothing and there was no reply when he telephoned the gendarme officer's home.

The carefully planned operation was close to unravelling, but Henri was determined to carry on. He had to; this was Paul and Jean-Pierre's only chance of escape.

While Henri went through operational details with Léon, Paul took the opportunity to sneak out for a closer look at Didier's motorbike.

It had two wheels, handlebars and an engine, but the similarities with the one he'd ridden in Antwerp ended there. Paul's machine had been pedal-started – basically a bicycle with a small engine – and once it was running there were only the throttle and the brakes to consider. Didier's was a serious motorbike, with kick-start, choke, clutch and gears to manipulate and master.

Paul did, in theory, know how to get a bike like this running. A friend of his father's had a motorbike and had once demonstrated how to start and ride it. Paul had even tried using the kick-start. But that was as far as it went.

Paul hadn't mentioned any of this to Henri, Josette and Léon.

They were all watching as he buttoned his jacket, pulled on gloves and slipped a pair of goggles over his head. He walked to the bike, trying to recall the three words his father's friend had used when telling him how to start the engine. He'd used these three words several times; Paul knew they were important, but he was struggling to remember them.

Josette came closer. "Good luck, Paul," she said softly. "Come back safely."

Paul's eyes were fixed on the bike. Suddenly he turned to Josette. "Compression, spark, fuel."

"What?"

"Something just came back to me." He smiled. "See you later."

Muttering "compression, spark, fuel," Paul casually eased out the kick-start and gently pumped it with his right boot, trying to make it look as though he'd done it a hundred times before. Soon he felt the slight resistance, what his dad's friend had called the "compression stroke". Phase one was successfully completed. Now he had to prime the engine with oil before switching on the fuel and ignition. He pushed down hard with his boot, then again, and a third time; so far so good. He switched on the fuel, choke and ignition and, after a reassuring smile in the general direction of his audience, he kicked down again.

The engine coughed, then spluttered, but didn't start.

Paul took a deep breath and reapplied his foot. Another splutter but still the bike didn't start.

"Come on," Paul whispered, his head down. "Please, don't do this."

"Be careful you don't flood the engine," Léon said.

Paul nodded, pushed the choke in a little and tried once more. The engine gave another cough, as though it were clearing its throat, and this time burst into life.

With a whispered murmur of thanks, Paul gently feathered the throttle and swung his leg over the machine. He fitted the goggles onto his eyes, gripped the handlebars and eased the bike off its stand. Then he carefully shut off the choke so that he was controlling the engine with the throttle.

He'd got it started; now all he had to do was make it move.

"See you in Rivel," he said to Henri.

Henry pointed to the front of the bike, mouthing over the noise. "Lights."

Lights. He had forgotten the lights! He flicked the switch and the area in front of the house was suddenly illuminated. He kicked the bike into gear. It lurched forward as he eased out the clutch, almost stalling. He quickly pulled the clutch back in and smiled at Henri. "Just getting used to the gears."

Henri nodded, looking far from convinced.

Paul tried again and the bike edged forward. The movement was still jerky, but this time he rode unsteadily to the open gates, with Josette, Henri and Léon scuttling after him.

As they watched, Paul wobbled away down the dimly lit street. They heard a clunk as he changed gear, but the bike kept moving, weaving from side to side before it finally rounded a bend and disappeared.

Léon turned to Henri. "Are you sure he's ridden a motor-bike before?"

The first couple of minutes were pretty scary as the bike stuttered along, and Paul feared that at any moment he would end up lying on his backside in the middle of the road with the machine stalled and damaged beyond riding.

But he was a quick learner, and soon, despite some over-revving and a few more sudden jerks, he had mastered the clutch and gears and was riding more confidently, grateful to have made it away from the house in one piece.

The road was almost arrow-straight to begin with, and largely protected from the wind by buildings on both sides. But after a kilometre or so, Paul left the town's boundaries and the valley opened up.

The fierce wind, which had been building all day, now toyed with him, attacking first from one side and then the other. But Paul clung on, and as the road began to drop downwards, steep banks and trees provided some respite. Soon he was negotiating a series of tight, twisting bends, carefully leaning into each turn. He thought of Father Lagarde, the way he drove the Bugatti as though he were part of it, and tried to become part of the motorbike.

He reached the village of L'Aiguillion, where he had to make a left turn. So far there had been no traffic in either direction, exactly as he had hoped. Once he turned onto the smaller road the chance of meeting another vehicle was even less. Without having to stop, he completed the turn.

There were high hills to his left and to his immediate right he glimpsed the river, mirroring the course of the road. Less than a mile later he was turning again, crossing a bridge to head up into the village of Lesparrou.

The streets were empty; the shutters all closed. There was no sign of life until, passing the last house on the main street, Paul heard dogs barking furiously at the sound of the engine.

The road dropped downwards, narrowing further, and Paul recalled from his trip with Didier that from now on it would be little more than a track.

As he moved into the open valley, the wind attacked again, this time from all sides at once. Buffeted and blasted, Paul dropped a gear and accelerated, more confident now.

The valley was wide at this point, the road rising and falling like a switchback, but Paul kept his eyes and his concentration on the way ahead.

Now the bike entered thick forest, with tall pines and wind-whipped ferns crowding in from both sides. Waving branches and shifting foliage made fantastic shapes and patterns as they were caught fleetingly in the headlight's beam.

Paul forced himself to ignore everything; all that mattered was reaching Rivel. He leaned into every snaking twist and turn as, on either side of him, the wind howled through the trees, dominating even the roar of the bike.

Suddenly, just ahead in the middle of the road and frozen

in the beam, Paul saw a bulky shape, like a crouched man ready to pounce.

Two narrow, malevolent eyes glared through the darkness.

Paul jammed on the brakes, too hard, too fast, and the rear wheel slid round to the left, propelling the bike closer and closer to the hunched shape in the road.

Paul's right foot instinctively went to the ground as he battled to stay upright. Releasing some of the pressure on the brakes, he wrenched at the handlebars and managed to straighten the bike and bring it to a standstill.

A huge, shaggy wild boar stood a few metres away, its black eyes gleaming, two stunted, creamy tusks pointed directly at Paul.

This close, the animal was terrifying. It glared and grunted, lowering its head, the hairs on its back rising and stiffening as it snorted loudly, challenging, threatening.

Paul was certain the beast was preparing to charge, ready to do battle. He had to respond to the challenge.

"No!" he shouted. "You're not stopping me! I'm coming through!"

The animal snorted again, streams of thick snot oozing from its fleshy snout.

"Get out of my way!" Paul yelled as he shoved the bike into gear and wound up the throttle, revving the engine wildly.

The animal charged. The bike hurtled forward.

It was like a game of chicken, and it was over in seconds. At the very last moment, it was the boar that chickened out, swerving to its right with a furious squeal and crashing through the roadside trees and into the forest.

"Yes!" Paul screamed into the night. "Yes!"

He roared on, and he didn't look back.

Breaking clear of the woodland, Paul crossed a bridge and was surprised to find himself in Rivel. It was as though the village had ducked out of sight, not wanting to be seen from a distance.

Paul had got through; he'd done it. He slowed the bike but didn't stop, passing through the village and continuing along a straight road fringed on both sides by plane trees. He took a right turn and, soon after, pulled into the clearing where he was to meet Henri and Léon.

There was no sign of the truck. Paul circled the bike so that he was facing the road, came to a halt and switched off the engine and lights.

He sat back and released a huge sigh of relief. Lifting the goggles, he rubbed his eyes and then checked his watch. It was ten minutes to eleven, the journey had taken no more than fifty minutes, but it felt like hours.

Paul pulled the bike onto its stand, got off and walked tentatively around the clearing. His body ached; his muscles were tight with tension.

Something snapped nearby and Paul stopped dead,

tensing. He peered into the enveloping darkness, wondering if hostile eyes were watching him; another wild boar, perhaps, or worse, human eyes. But apart from the swaying branches, nothing moved.

Paul relaxed.

Soon after eleven he heard the truck approaching. He watched, relieved, as it swung into the clearing, stopping beneath the canopy of a tall tree, well hidden from the road.

The headlights went out and Henri and Léon jumped down from the cab.

"Well done, Paul, you made it," Henri said, grasping his hand and pumping it energetically. "Any problems?"

Paul paused briefly and then shook his head. "Problems? No, not really."

THIRTY-THREE

Two dismal floodlights did almost nothing to illuminate the camp. Large areas were in deep shadow or total darkness, the outline of the four low blocks, where two hundred and fifty or more prisoners were housed, just visible in the gloom.

A dim light burned from the central guardhouse, but there had been no sign of movement in the twenty minutes Henri and Léon had spent watching, crouched outside the wire fence on the south side of the camp, well away from the road.

The wind had dropped swiftly to next to nothing, as it often did this close to the mountains. An occasional feeble gust ruffled the treetops, a half-hearted reminder of the earlier ferocious force that swept through the valley.

Now the night was still and virtually silent. Every so often Henri and Léon caught the sound of a hacking cough or muffled groan from the closest hut, but that was all. There had been no sign of patrolling guards.

Henri checked his watch, the luminous hands and numerals glowing brightly in the darkness. It was twenty minutes to twelve.

"We should cut the wire now," he whispered.

Léon nodded and watched as Henri took the wire-cutters and snipped through the first strand.

The snap of the metal sounded deafening. Both men froze, expecting to hear shouts and see armed guards running towards them. But nothing happened.

When he was certain the noise had not given them away, Henri turned to Léon. "I don't have a gun with me," he whispered. "Do you?"

"No," Léon answered. "And I wouldn't know how use one anyway."

Henri laughed softly. "Fine freedom fighters we are."

Léon took off his scarf and handed it to Henri. "Hold this over the wire when you cut, it might help muffle the noise. And try not to slice through it; it was a present from my wife."

Cautiously, Henri made the next cut. The scarf did help deaden the sound.

"I've never been much of a fighter," Léon said quietly as he watched Henri work. "I just take people from one place to another."

"It all counts, my friend."

"I hope so. Seeing this place close up makes you wonder though."

Henry cut through another strand. "Wonder what?"

"Why no one has tried to escape before. Slack guards, little security; it wouldn't be difficult."

Henri stopped cutting and looked at him. "Léon, the men in there are not criminals. They're not in there for anything they've done, it's just because of who they are. Most of them are probably still thinking this is all a big mistake and that soon they'll be set free and allowed to return to their families."

He went back to work and within a couple of minutes had cut a gap big enough for a man to slip through.

They sat and waited. Time passed painfully slowly. Henri repeatedly checked his watch.

Twelve o'clock came. And went.

Both men were afraid even to consider the possibility that Jean-Pierre was not coming.

The minutes dragged on. Three minutes past the hour, six minutes past. Henri silently decided that if Jean-Pierre had not arrived at the fence by a quarter past they would have to return to Lavelanet without him.

Then there was a slight, almost inaudible sound from the closest hut. A door creaked and seconds later two shadowy figures appeared through the gloom.

They watched as one figure helped the other, moving along the side of the hut and into open ground. Soon they reached the fence.

Henri had never met the guard, but knew he was Gaston

Rouzard's contact, Raymond Martel. He nodded an acknowledgement and then almost gasped at the sight of Jean-Pierre. He looked ill. Frail and gaunt.

"What's wrong with him?" Henri asked Martel.

Martel shrugged. "Dysentery, for one thing. It's his own fault. What can he expect if he keeps getting thrown into the cell?"

"Can he walk?"

"Of course I can walk, Henri," Jean-Pierre said, his voice as weak as his body. "And I can hear and speak too."

"I'm sorry, Jean-Pierre," Henri said quickly. "Forgive me."

Jean-Pierre managed a smile. "I'll forgive you anything if you get me away from this place."

"What about the other prisoners?" Léon said to Martel. "Did any of them see you bring him out?"

Martel gave another shrug, apparently unconcerned. "They know better than to say anything."

"The other guards then?"

"Asleep."

With Henri's help, Jean-Pierre crawled through the gap in the wire, wheezing and stifling a cough.

Henri turned back to Martel. "I suppose Gaston told you that you'll receive the rest of your money when our operation is completed."

Martel grinned. "Yes, he told me, just before he passed out."

"Passed out?"

"He had a few too many glasses of red wine while we were reminiscing, missed the last train back and is sleeping it off at my place. He was snoring like a pig when I left to come on duty."

Henri nodded. The mystery of Gaston's failure to return to Lavelanet was explained.

Jean-Pierre coughed again, louder this time, and Martel took a quick glance at the guardhouse. "I'd better go back." He nodded towards Jean-Pierre. "Get him away now. He should be all right in a few days."

Henri had told Paul they expected to have Jean-Pierre back at the clearing in just over an hour. They had moved off soon after eleven and as Paul checked his watch again he saw that half past midnight had come and gone.

Unable to rest, never mind doze as Henri had suggested, he had paced the clearing, wide awake, buzzing, focused on the task ahead: getting Jean-Pierre back to Lavelanet.

Although midnight had come and gone, they were only in phase one of the operation. It was going to be a long night.

Paul checked the bike, making sure everything was still in order. Then he circled the truck, giving it the once over, even though he didn't really know what he was looking for.

He glanced at his watch again and walked to the front of the clearing, close to the road. Immediately he spotted a pinprick of light.

A torch; they were coming.

"This is our friend, Paul," Henri said to Jean-Pierre as they entered the clearing. "He's going to take you back to Lavelanet."

Jean-Pierre nodded, his voice little more than a hoarse whisper as he spoke. "Thank you, Paul, I'm very grateful."

Paul stared, lost for words. At last, he was face to face with the man he had heard about ever since his arrival. He'd expected some sort of heroic figure – big, strong, bursting with pride and energy – but the young man standing here looked broken and defeated. Even in those few seconds Paul couldn't help thinking there was no way Jean-Pierre would be capable of walking over the mountains.

Henri must have read his thoughts. "I've explained to Jean-Pierre that you both have a long journey ahead," he said quickly. "He's suffering from dysentery, but we'll get him cleaned up and give him plenty of water to drink and he'll be fine."

Paul nodded, but said nothing.

"Time to go," Henri continued. "And remember, Paul, not to the safe house we spoke about at the meeting last night. Go to the other place."

THIRTY-FOUR

Josette could not disguise her relief and joy as she heard the motorbike pull up outside her grandmother's house. She leapt from her chair, rushed to the front door and yanked it open.

Paul was helping Jean-Pierre off the bike. Josette stared, hardly believing how much the young man had changed.

Somehow, though, he managed a smile. "Ah, the young lady from the café," he muttered.

"I'm Henri's daughter," Josette said as brightly as she could, standing aside so that Paul could help him into the house.

Jean-Pierre laughed. "I might have known. You should have told me…"

Whatever he was about to add was lost as the coughing began, a raking, painful cough rooted deep in his chest.

Josette followed them inside. Odile stood waiting by the door to the kitchen.

"Gra-mere, this is Jean-Pierre…"

"I know who he is," Odile said, taking his hand. "You need water, plenty of water, and a bath and change of clothes. And then there's a meal of cassoulet for you both."

Jean-Pierre forced another smile. "My favourite. How did you know?"

Before Odile could answer he spoke again. "But I'm afraid that before anything, I must go … I must use…"

"Yes," Odile said to save his embarrassment. "Come with me. And drink some water first. It will help."

As Jean-Pierre walked unsteadily towards the kitchen, Odile looked over at Paul. "We're very proud of you, for what you did tonight," she said simply before following Jean-Pierre out of the room.

As soon as the door closed, Josette turned to Paul. "What's wrong with him?"

"Your father said it's dysentery. I don't know much about it, but it affects the stomach. That's why he—"

"Yes, I see," Josette said, interrupting.

"But the cough is something else."

"Will he get better?"

"He says he will. He says he's ready for the long walk across the mountains."

"But he looks awful." Josette was studying Paul's face. "And you look tired. How was it?"

Paul decided not to mention his encounter with the wild boar. "Getting there was … interesting. The wind made handling the bike difficult, but it dropped by the time we started back so it was a lot easier. My biggest worry was that Jean-Pierre would let go of my waist and fall off." He shrugged. "But we made it. Is there any news about Didier?"

"I telephoned the hospital again. He's still sleeping."

"I wish I could see him before … before I leave."

Josette nodded and then suddenly looked shy. "We are, you know."

"You are?" Paul said, confused. "Are what?"

"What Gra-mere told you – proud of what you did tonight."

Paul was as unused to receiving compliments from Josette as she was to giving them. They stood in an awkward silence.

"When will Papa be back?" Josette asked eventually.

"Soon, I guess. Their route takes a little longer, and I was much quicker on the way back. They have to take the truck to the yard and bring their cars here, so it might be … it could be … I don't know really."

He was floundering, saying too much, but nothing of what he wanted to say. He knew that once Henri and Léon arrived at the cottage, he would be on the road again, after saying goodbye to Josette for the final time.

"I wish I hadn't been so horrible to you when you first got here," Josette said. "It was such a waste of time."

Paul smiled. "You weren't that horrible."

"I was. And … and the thing is … well…" Josette was floundering too. "I do like you. You're very nice."

"You're … you're very nice too."

They fell silent again. The silence felt loud in the small sitting room.

"I wish you were staying," Josette said at last.

Paul didn't respond, even when Josette raised her eyebrows and nodded at him, indicating that it was his turn to speak.

She sighed. "And now you're supposed to say that you wish you were staying too."

"I do wish I could stay," Paul said. "But I'm not saying it because … it's impossible. I can't, even though I'd like to … and…"

They were standing close together, looking into each other's eyes.

Josette leaned a little closer, and then Paul did. Josette moved closer still. Paul hesitated; this wasn't meant to happen. But now their faces were just inches apart and Paul saw Josette's eyes closing, and noticed her beautiful long eyelashes. His own eyes were closing. He felt himself swallow, certain that Josette must have heard the ridiculous sound it made. But it didn't matter. The next second her lips were brushing against his.

The door to the kitchen opened.

"Josette … oh!"

Odile lifted one hand to her mouth, realizing what she had interrupted.

"What is it, Gra-mere?" Josette said quickly, her face crimson.

"No, nothing, I was going to ask… It doesn't matter."

"But I want to help. What can I do?"

"I was only going to ask you to take the cassoulet from the oven while I help Jean-Pierre wash and change."

"Is he all right?"

"Yes, a little better, but I can manage…"

"I'll do it," Josette said, hurrying past her grandmother into the kitchen.

Odile sighed, smiled apologetically at Paul and shrugged her shoulders. "Sorry," she whispered.

Jean-Pierre had a bit more colour in his cheeks, but he was still only picking at the cassoulet. The heavy stew of sausage, duck and white haricot beans was meant to set them up for the long walk ahead. Paul was also eating sparingly; so was Josette. Odile wondered silently if this was the least successful meal she had ever cooked, when her son, Henri, stuck his head around the kitchen door and beamed at them.

"That smells delicious. Is there enough for two late-comers?"

"More than enough," Odile said, getting up to fetch plates from a tall wooden cabinet.

Henri and Léon sat down.

"How are you feeling now?" Henri asked Jean-Pierre.

"Much better," Jean-Pierre said. "And looking forward to my little stroll in the hills with Paul."

"Good, good," Henri said encouragingly. But Paul noticed the concerned look that passed between Henri and Léon.

"And Didier," Henri asked, "how is he?"

"Sleeping," Paul and Josette said together and then shared an embarrassed smile.

"Good, good," Henri said again.

"The nurse I spoke to said other people had phoned to ask about him," Josette added.

"Which people?"

"I didn't ask. Is it important?"

Henry shook his head. "Perhaps, I'm not sure."

Odile set down two more plates of steaming cassoulet.

Léon smiled. "The taste of the Languedoc," he said, picking up his knife and fork. "Marvellous."

But Henri was unable to switch off his thoughts. "I felt sure we'd be stopped on the way back from Rivel. But there was nothing; no delays, no gendarmes. We saw three cars during the entire journey. It doesn't make sense, unless…"

"Unless what, Papa?" Josette asked.

"Unless Didier *did* just fall into the machine," said Henri, thinking aloud.

"Papa, what do you mean?"

Henri realized he had said more than he'd intended. "Nothing, eat your cassoulet."

"Papa!"

"I'm sorry, Josette," Henri said and then decided to voice his fears. "When Gaston didn't return from Chalabre I was afraid that he had betrayed us. With Didier out of the way he'd know I would continue with the operation, but use the truck instead of the motorbike. It would have been simple then to have the gendarmes arrest us once we'd freed Jean-Pierre from Rivel. Léon and I would have been caught red-handed."

"But Gaston didn't know Paul could ride the motorbike," Josette said quickly.

"Exactly," her father said. "The point is we *weren't* stopped; we saw no one. It seems my suspicions of Gaston are unfounded. According to the guard at Rivel, he's just sleeping off too much red wine back in Chalabre."

Paul was following Henri's reasoning closely. "And Gaston couldn't have pushed Didier, as he was on the train when it happened. Even if he *is* involved he would have to have an accomplice at the factory."

"I've considered that too," Henri said, with a sad shake of the head.

Léon looked up from his cassoulet. "We've often said that it's difficult to know who to trust these days."

"It's true," Henri agreed. "But I've always thought of Gaston as a true patriot."

"Henri," Odile said quietly, "remember that there are many ways of expressing patriotism. And not all patriots think as we do."

Henri nodded. "You're right, Maman," he said with a smile. "As always. I know in my heart that Didier *was* pushed. And I know it was because of his involvement in the operation."

They continued the meal in a thoughtful silence. When it was finished Odile got up from the table and began to clear away the dishes.

"I've packed food and bottles of water," she said to Henri. "The food should last for some time." She looked at Jean-Pierre. "When you get high up, there are plenty of mountain springs. Drink as much as you can."

He nodded.

Henri checked his watch and pushed back his chair. "We must leave. We're due to meet the mountain team in an hour and a half."

"I'll lead in my car," Léon said, as he too stood. "You follow with Paul and Jean-Pierre."

Jean-Pierre got unsteadily to his feet, and Odile moved quickly to his side. "I'll walk out with you," she said, leading him by the arm to the doorway. She turned back to Josette. "Make sure Paul has all the food and drink safely with him before you two come out."

Josette stared at her grandmother. Odile was giving them the chance of a few moments together. For a last farewell.

The door closed and they stood facing each other, hesitating, uncertain. They had only seconds but both seemed unable to move.

Tentatively, Paul reached out and took Josette's hands in his. He gently pulled her towards him and this time they did kiss. Not for long, but for long enough.

Then Josette took a tiny backwards step, her eyes moist with tears.

"I'll never forget you, Paul," she whispered.

THIRTY-FIVE

The two cars ploughed through the deep black of the early morning hours, Henri peering studiously through the windscreen as the tail-lights of Léon's car continually disappeared and then reappeared as they took one tight bend after another.

They were heading for a rendezvous point on the southern side of Saint-Girons, a town about the same size as Lavelanet. It sat close to where a number of trails headed into the mountains towards Spain.

Paul could see just enough to notice that the ever-changing landscape had altered yet again. They were no longer in a terrain of hills and wide valleys. Now they were in the mountains, with twisting roads winding constantly upward, and towering peaks looming ever nearer.

Jean-Pierre was asleep in the rear seat, with Paul in the front, next to Henri. Paul couldn't sleep, although it was already three o'clock. His thoughts kept returning to Josette and the knowledge that he would never see her again.

He spoke quietly with Henri, partly to keep his mind off Josette, and partly to help Henri stay alert as he negotiated hairpin corners where terrifying descents lurked dangerously close to the roadside.

They spoke of Belgium, and then Henri asked Paul about his earlier life in England. Paul remembered it fondly, talking about his school and former friends. But even as he spoke he felt that his time in England had been like another life, almost another world.

And he knew, too, that he didn't want to return there. Perhaps that would change later, but for now he didn't want to go back. There was nothing and no one for him in England. No family, not even a distant relative.

As he stared ahead, seeing the lights of Léon's car come into view again, he realized that the people he felt closest to were the ones he'd been living and working for during these past couple of weeks. And he was desperately worried about all of them.

He had to voice his fears. "If there are traitors in Lavelanet it means that even after Jean-Pierre and I have gone, you and Didier will still be in danger. And possibly Josette too."

Henri negotiated the next hairpin bend and then nodded. "We're at war, Paul. In wartime everyone is in danger in some way or another."

They passed through Saint-Girons and then turned towards the smaller town of Seix.

The two vehicles climbed steadily higher and Jean-Pierre sat up, rubbing his eyes. "I feel better for a sleep," he said, yawning. The yawn quickly changed to a barking cough.

Henri glanced at Jean-Pierre's face reflected in the rear-view mirror, seeing at once that he still looked pale and drawn.

"Don't worry, Henri, I'll be OK," Jean-Pierre said, when the coughing had stopped. "I'll keep drinking water, that's what your mother told me." He laughed. "We're going to England, eh, Paul? Maybe they'll allow me a little holiday before I join General de Gaulle. Perhaps you'll have time to show me the Tower of London."

"I hope so," Paul answered. It was the second time the London landmark had been mentioned since the start of his flight to freedom. The Tower of London appeared to hold the same fascination for the French as the Eiffel Tower in Paris did for the English. Paul had never seen either.

Léon's car began to slow and then pulled off the road, coming to a halt on the edge of a small hamlet. Henri stopped his own vehicle directly behind and they climbed quietly out into the night.

They were outside a small café with a faded sign above the door. Its windows were shuttered; the place appeared to be in total darkness.

"We have to go around to the back," Léon whispered.

Stepping carefully past crates of empty bottles, they trooped to the back of the building, where a light burned behind closed curtains. Léon tapped gently on the door and they heard a chair scrape across a tiled floor.

The door opened slightly and a small, balding man peered through the gap.

"Ah, Léon," he said, "you've arrived. Come in, come in."

One by one they filed silently into the kitchen.

The café owner was called Jacques. Léon quickly made the introductions.

"A slight change of plan," Jacques said, after shaking hands with everyone. He spotted the anxious looks on the faces of the newcomers. "No, nothing for you to worry about. One of the original team has been hurt. A hunting accident. It seems a cartridge from his shotgun blew back in his face. No one can understand how it happened. Poor fellow might lose his sight. So we have a different team; they offered to take over."

"Do you know them?" Léon asked.

Jacques gave a shrug. "No, I don't know them personally. But they know the man who was hurt; one of them was with him when the accident happened. And they obviously know what they're doing. Proper mountain men – told me they've made the crossing many times, by the Eagle Trail and others."

Léon turned to Henri. "Is this all right with you?"

It wasn't all right; it was another hitch. But Henri had coped with many hitches during that long day and this one didn't appear to threaten the operation.

"They know the financial arrangement?" he asked Jacques.

"Yes, they know the deal; half the money now and half when your friends are in Spain. They told me they'd give some to the man who was hurt, so they must be all right. They're all prepared, but they won't leave until after first light, when it's safe."

Henri hesitated for a moment longer before nodding. "I'm sure it will be fine," he said to Paul and Jean-Pierre.

"They're in the bar," the café owner said. "You'd better come through and meet them." He paused. "Oh, by the way, they're a quiet lot; don't say very much. And you won't find them easy to understand. They're Andorrans."

THIRTY-SIX

It was almost five o'clock when Henri's car crested the hill on the approach to Lavelanet. The first streaks of daylight were appearing, like small rips in the black sky.

Henri had passed tiredness. His mind was racing, his thoughts tumbling and he was unable to shake off the powerful sense of unease he'd felt since encountering the three Andorrans.

They were a quiet lot, as the café owner had said. But from the moment he set eyes on them, Henri felt there was more to it than that. They were brooding and surly, particularly their leader, who was hard-faced and short-necked, and built like a bull.

When Henri and the others had walked through to the café bar, the Andorrans didn't get to their feet but remained seated around a table, nursing small glasses of spirit and smoking foul-smelling cigarettes, their shotguns resting against the nearby wall.

The leader managed a nod when Jacques introduced

Léon and Henri, but he appeared more interested in weighing up Paul and Jean-Pierre once he heard they were the two he was about to escort to Spain.

"What's wrong with him?" he growled to Henri in fractured French as he watched Jean-Pierre slump into a chair at another table.

"There's nothing wrong with me," Jean-Pierre answered before Henri could reply. "A bit of stomach trouble, that's all. Nothing that need hold us up."

The Andorran grunted, shrugged his shoulders and muttered something to his friends in what sounded to Henri like a mixture of Catalan, Spanish and French.

His failure to understand only increased his sense of unease. The feeling didn't diminish as he handed over half the fee, nor when he watched the man slowly count each note, nor when he reminded him that Paul would give him the second half once they crossed the border into Spain.

He saw the man's eyes flick greedily onto Paul and linger there before sliding down to the small case in which the money was locked.

The Andorran pocketed the cash and went back to his drink, his cigarette and his friends, disinterested in anything further Henri had to say. The deal was done; business was concluded.

With a nagging feeling of doubt, Henri said his good-byes, first to Jean-Pierre and then Paul, embracing them both, trying to summon up brave, encouraging words to speed them on their way. But the heroic sentiments would not come and in the end he could manage nothing more stirring than, "Goodbye, my young friends, and good luck."

In response, Jean-Pierre said, "Goodbye, Henri, and you, Léon. I'll return with the General."

Paul had said quite a few goodbyes over the past three weeks and this one was almost as difficult as his farewell to Josette. He solemnly shook hands with Léon and then turned to Henri. There was so much to say but finally Paul, too, was lost for adequate words.

"Thank you, Henri," he murmured, gripping his hand tightly. "Thank you. I'll be back one day too."

Henri nodded, looking as though he had more to say, but then hurried away, saying nothing.

For the entire return journey, through Saint-Girons and towards Foix, where he waved goodbye to Léon, and then dropping down into Lavelanet, Henri's feeling of unease increased. Leaving Paul and Jean-Pierre with the Andorrans just hadn't felt right, but there was nothing more he could do.

Josette had remained at her grandmother's, so instead of going straight home, Henri drove to Odile's cottage to collect her. As he drew up he saw Didier's motorbike still parked outside and made a mental note to do something about getting it moved in the morning.

He climbed wearily from the driver's seat and stood in the road stretching, his body stiff from the journey. He rolled his head all the way around his shoulders in one direction and then the other, groaning as the tiny bones in his neck clicked and shifted into place.

With a long sigh, he took out the key to his mother's house he had always kept. He unlocked the door as quietly as possible, thinking that Odile and Josette would both be asleep.

As soon as he stepped inside he heard voices coming from the kitchen. They were speaking quietly, as though trying not to disturb the stillness of the early morning. But even so, from the low pitch, Henri was certain that one of the speakers was a man. His thoughts instantly turned to Gaston Rouzard. He must have returned from Chalabre after all.

There was much Henri wanted to say to Gaston and even more he wanted to hear.

He strode to the kitchen, pushed open the door and then stared in surprise.

Didier, bandaged, bruised and battered, was sitting at the table with Odile and Josette.

"Hello, Henri," he said with the slightest of smiles. "I have to talk to you."

"Didier," Henri gasped.

"I'm all right," Didier said, "I discharged myself. They didn't want me to leave but I had to tell you what I've remembered."

"But what about your head?"

"A bit of concussion, that's all."

"And your arm and—"

"Papa!" Josette said impatiently. "You must listen to Didier!"

"Sit down, Henri," Odile said. "I'll get you some coffee."

"Thank you," Henri said, sinking onto a chair and nodding to Didier to continue.

"First of all," Didier said, "you must know that I was pushed. I couldn't remember when I first came around; I couldn't remember anything. Then I was asleep and it all came back to me. At first I didn't know if I was awake or asleep; if what I was seeing really happened. But now I'm sure. I remember everything."

"I knew it was no accident," Henri said. "Who did it?"

"The one person in the factory who knows the machines almost as well as I do."

"You mean Marcel?"

Didier shook his head. "No, not Marcel. Yvette."

Henri gasped.

"I saw her," Didier continued. "I turned slightly as I fell. She was glaring at me with a look in her eyes I'd never seen before. Not hatred, it was as though she was ... possessed; as though she had to do it."

"Yvette," Henri breathed, almost to himself. "I never considered ... not seriously." He turned back to Didier. "You're absolutely certain about this?"

"There's no doubt at all, Henri. I saw her as plainly as I

see you now. And our eyes met; she knew I'd seen her." He flinched slightly as a stab of pain shot through his arm and shoulder. "She's always teased me that she knows the machines better than I do. And she was clever; disconnected the wires knowing I'd think they had come apart by accident. It's happened before – someone snagging them, or the effect of the vibrations. She knew I'd spot it quickly and then lean over the drive belt to reconnect them."

Henri cupped both hands around the mug of steaming coffee Odile had placed on the table. "I can hardly believe it."

"She must have been watching from the corner," Didier continued. "Once I reconnected the wires all she had to do was flick the 'on' switch and give me a shove. She could have been spotted, but she obviously thought it worth the risk."

The hot coffee almost scalded Henri's throat as he swallowed. "I'll go to see her now," he said. "Confront her; find out who put her up to it."

Didier glanced quickly at Odile and Josette. "I'm afraid you're too late, Henri," he said.

"Too late?"

Didier nodded. "Yvette is dead."

THIRTY-SEVEN

Outside it was rapidly growing light. Didier's words thundered around Henri's mind, thudding and crashing against his ever-growing fears for Paul and Jean-Pierre.

"Tell me," he said to Didier. "Tell me, quickly."

Didier shifted awkwardly on his chair, clearly still in pain. He took a deep breath. "I went to her house, to confront her myself; try to find out why she did it. I always thought she liked me. She knew my mother—"

"But what happened?" Henri urged.

"Henri, calm down," Odile said gently. "He's still badly shaken."

Henri hesitated, afraid to explain his deeper fears to his mother and Josette. It was as though he held a tangled ball of string in his hands. Each newly unravelled strand took him a little closer to the truth, but not quickly enough, because with every passing second he grew more certain that Paul and Jean-Pierre were in danger.

"I'm sorry," he said to Didier. "Take your time."

"Her house is near ours and on a terraced street like ours," Didier said. "I knocked at the front door; there were lights on but she didn't come. I knocked again, but no answer."

"And then?"

Didier took the glass of water Odile offered him, nodding his thanks. "The only access to the back of the house is by the passageway that runs behind the terrace; our street is the same. But to get to the passageway, you have to go to the end of the street and then around to the back. It took a few minutes. I couldn't run, and anyway, I didn't think there was any need to hurry."

He paused for a sip of water. Henri tried not to show his impatience.

"It was dark at the back," Didier continued, putting down the glass, "and I wasn't sure which house was which; I'd never been along that passageway. But a light was on in one, and then I saw Yvette's bicycle against the wall. She rides it to work – there's a broken basket on the front."

"So you saw her?"

Didier nodded. "Yes, I crept to the window and I saw her; in a chair, but slumped over the table with her head towards the window. Dead. Her eyes were wide open; staring. If I'd got there a little sooner, maybe…"

"It would have made no difference, Didier," Henri said.

"But you don't understand – it might have," Didier said quickly. "When I saw Yvette, I also saw someone move behind her, the door to the room being pulled shut. It was the murderer; it had to be. I tried the back door but it was locked. He must have gone out through the front door, where I'd been a few minutes earlier. He would have heard me knocking."

Henri said nothing, his mind churning again. As soon as Didier mentioned Yvette's murderer, he had once again thought of Gaston Rouzard. He was the obvious suspect, the only suspect. Henri's suspicions kept returning to Gaston.

But Gaston was in Chalabre. He couldn't have killed Yvette, unless the camp guard Raymond Martel had been lying.

"Papa," Josette said, breaking into Henri's thoughts, "what about Paul and Jean-Pierre? Did everything go as planned?"

Henri sighed. "Not exactly. One of the original team had an accident with a gun, so another team have taken over. Andorrans."

"And you're worried about it, I can see you are," Josette said.

"I don't know, just something. It didn't feel right." He smiled wearily at his daughter. "Nothing feels quite right. I'm probably overtired."

Odile stood up. "Go home; get some sleep. All of you."

No one moved, so Odile shrugged her shoulders and went to the stove. "I'll make some more coffee."

"You know," Didier said after a few moments, "Yvette was from Andorra."

"What?" Henri said.

"I remember my mother telling me. Yvette married old Armand Bigou; he died a few years ago. He was much older than Yvette, by at least twenty years."

"I don't remember that," Henri said frowning.

"My mother told me there was a joke that went around for a while. The story was that Armand went to Andorra in search of a job but came back with a young wife instead. Then he sent her to work in the factory while he stayed at home doing nothing."

"Yes … yes…" Henri murmured, "I do remember now. I'd completely forgotten."

"I suppose she must still have family up there in the mountains," Didier said. "Or friends."

Henri stared. And then he sprang to his feet.

"Papa, what's wrong?"

"I'm going back."

"Back? Back where?"

"I'm going after Paul and Jean-Pierre. I've felt it all along; they're in danger. I should never have left them. This, all this, is connected in some way. I've got to help."

Didier stood up. "Then I'm coming with you."

"No, Didier, you're in no condition for it. You'd only slow me down."

"Let me come," Josette said. "If they're really in danger—"

"No!" Henri snapped. "You stay here, Josette, and that's final, no arguments."

"But—"

"I said no arguments!" Henri sounded and looked furious. And he was. Furious with himself, and furious at not trusting his own instincts. He turned to Odile. "Do you still have my father's old shotgun?"

"Yes, but it hasn't been fired for years."

"I have a shotgun," Didier said. "It works perfectly. Let me—"

"No, Didier!" Henri snapped again. "Cartridges?" he said to Odile.

"I think there's a box. But they're probably useless by now."

"Fetch them for me, please. And hurry."

THIRTY-EIGHT

Jean-Pierre was coughing uncontrollably, bent almost double with one hand against a tree trunk for support. Paul watched helplessly, while the three Andorrans looked on with openly hostile stares.

They had been walking for just over two hours and progress was slow. It was a bright, crisp morning and the sun climbed steadily into a cloudless sky. But the thinning air seemed only to increase the vice-like tightness gripping Jean-Pierre's chest.

Finally, the coughing stopped. Jean-Pierre stood slowly upright and with a nod of thanks took the bottle of water Paul offered. He guzzled greedily, but too quickly, and the cool water in his raw, inflamed throat started another painful bout of coughing.

Paul grabbed the bottle and waited, and gradually the coughing subsided. He offered the water once more.

Jean-Pierre smiled weakly but shook his head. He wiped his face on the arm of his jacket. "I'm sorry about that," he said, looking towards the Andorrans. "I'll be all right in a minute or two."

The Andorrans looked on without sympathy, puffing on fat, rolled cigarettes and muttering to one another.

Jean-Pierre's eyes flicked apprehensively towards the track. It was getting much tougher.

For the first hour, the ascent had been gradual as they moved from woodland into open mountain valley. They saw no one, although the tinkling of bells heralded a meeting with a herd of twenty or more pale blond cows. One or two lifted their heads and cast baleful eyes on the passing walkers, but the rest ignored them and continued plodding on their way.

They trekked across the valley, taking a well-trodden and clearly marked path, which then forded a crystal-clear mountain stream. Soon the climb became harder, rising steeply, and Jean-Pierre began to struggle. His next coughing fit came as they reached a plunging waterfall, deep in a forested area.

After resting for a few minutes, a little of the colour returned to Jean-Pierre's face. He gazed at the cascading water and smiled. "Beautiful, eh, Paul? And such a lovely day for a walk."

He took the water bottle and drank again, much more cautiously this time. Then he turned and grinned at the sour-faced Andorrans. "Lead on, please, but not too quickly. My friend and I are enjoying the scenery."

The Andorrans said nothing. Each one had lit another

foul-smelling cigarette; they smoked almost constantly. At Jean-Pierre's words, the leader tossed his spittle-stained stub onto the mud track and ground it into the dirt. He gestured to his companions and they picked up their shotguns, slung them across their shoulders and stalked quickly onward, ignoring Jean-Pierre's request.

The narrow footpath wound steeply upwards through a dense forest of birch, ash and beech, which shut out much of the daylight. Exposed tree roots spread like raised veins across the path, and more than once in the dim light both Paul and Jean-Pierre tripped and almost fell.

Paul was tiring. He'd been awake for nearly twenty-four hours and the pumping adrenalin that had kept him going was finally running low. But he was fit and strong, and was coping physically, even though his hamstrings were tightening and beginning to ache, and his ankles were sore. He knew this was nothing compared to the pain and discomfort Jean-Pierre was enduring.

For all his suffering, Jean-Pierre did not utter one word of complaint. He battled on bravely, every so often rushing into the trees and emerging a few minutes later, using some of the precious water to wash his hands.

The Andorran leader complained that it was too soon for stops and that they must make up the lost time.

"What's the hurry?" Paul asked him testily as they waited again for Jean-Pierre. "My friend is ill, why can't we go slower?"

"Border guards and police," the Andorran grunted. He had finally admitted to the name of José after Paul had asked him several times. "Sometimes soldiers patrol the marked path. When the trail ends, then we go slower and rest. Only then. Then it is safe."

Paul was struggling to understand José. He was certain the Andorran spoke much more French than he was letting on.

And Paul wasn't convinced that he and Jean-Pierre would be safer once the trail disappeared. Their guides looked resolutely hostile. Paul didn't trust them.

The climb became even more testing when they broke clear of the forest. The ground underfoot was treacherous, packed mud was replaced by solid but slippery rock and jagged splinters and fallen scree shifting dangerously without warning.

But they were still following the marked trail.

And while Paul and Jean-Pierre slithered and stumbled, the Andorrans marched effortlessly on, as surefooted as mountain goats.

After another strenuous climb, Jean-Pierre came to a standstill, putting a hand on Paul's shoulder to steady himself. Beads of sweat stood out on his forehead, but he smiled at Paul and pointed skywards.

Paul stared up. High above, a huge bird with a massive wingspan circled majestically in the blue sky.

"A golden eagle," Jean-Pierre said, struggling for breath.

"Guiding us along the Eagle Trail," Paul said as he watched the bird soar.

Jean-Pierre managed a laugh. "Before the war, before this madness began, bird-watching was my interest. I know all the birds of southern France." He glanced again at the eagle. "The eagle was always my favourite. How quickly life changes, eh, Paul?"

The Andorrans had halted and were looking back.

"I need to rest for a little while," Jean-Pierre called to them.

"Again?" shouted José. "We stopped fifteen minutes ago. You said you would not hold us up."

"Give me a little longer this time," Jean-Pierre said. "I'll eat a little and drink some water, then I'll be all right."

"Look, if you want to get to Spain, you walk at our pace. I tell you, it is dangerous to stop now. Stop and start, it's pathetic."

"We'll walk at *our* pace!" Paul yelled in furious response. "You're being paid plenty for this job, so you'll do it the way we say!"

José glared, his eyes narrowing, and for moment Paul half expected all three guides to turn and stomp off into the mountains. Paul didn't notice as the leader's eyes flicked down to the little suitcase he was carrying.

The Andorran knew full well that the case contained much more than the remainder of their fee. He could be patient – he had to be while they were still in an area patrolled by guards. He shrugged his shoulders, nodded once to Paul and turned to his friends.

Jean-Pierre sank gratefully to the hard ground, resting his back against a large rock, breathing hard. He watched as Paul took the remaining water and some of the food from the shoulder bag Odile had packed for them.

Glancing quickly towards the Andorrans, Jean-Pierre leaned closer to Paul. "This isn't fair on you, Paul," he whispered. "My stomach is getting worse, and this cough… I'm very weak."

He sipped the water cautiously and sat back, suddenly looking completely drained and desperately tired. "I don't think I can make it."

"Eat this," Paul said, ignoring the comment and taking an apple from the bag. "It'll give you energy."

"You must listen to me, Paul," Jean-Pierre said urgently. "I don't think I have the strength to go on."

"But you do," Paul said equally forcefully. "I'll help you!" He took some cheese from the bag, broke off a small piece and handed that to Jean-Pierre too. "And anyway, you have to make it, we're going to see the Tower of London together, aren't we?"

Jean-Pierre smiled weakly and nodded. He took a bite of the apple and then leaned his head against the rock, staring into the sky, where the golden eagle continued to drift lazily.

The café was open but deserted apart from the owner, Jacques, who was seated behind the bar, a newspaper in his hands. He looked up, startled, as Henri flung open the door and rushed inside.

"Back again? Did you forget something?"

"How long ago did they leave?"

"Who?"

"My two friends, of course, and the Andorrans?"

The café owner shrugged. "A couple of hours; maybe a bit longer. That Jean-Pierre fellow didn't look too good. You want a coffee?"

"Where does the path start?"

"Which path?"

"The track leading to the Eagle Trail?"

"It's to the right of the café, about a hundred metres up the road."

"Is it easy to follow?"

"Simple enough to begin with," Jacques answered. "But once you get up high there's no marked trail. It's impossible to find the way unless you know it."

"I'll find the way."

"But you can't go up there without a guide. It's suicide. Stay and have a—"

But Henri had gone, leaving the door wide open as he rushed back to his car. He yanked open a rear door and pulled out the old shotgun, still in its canvas bag. He had already crammed the box of cartridges into his jacket pocket.

He slammed the door shut and hurried up the road.

THIRTY-NINE

Paul had refilled the bottles from a cool mountain spring. He was giving Jean-Pierre water as often as he could drink it, but it no longer seemed to help.

After the break for food Jean-Pierre had revived a little – but the recovery was brief. For the remainder of the morning and into the afternoon they stopped and started more and more frequently.

Now they had stopped again. Jean-Pierre was breathless and sweating, and Paul had reluctantly but silently accepted that his new friend could not walk for much longer.

Even the Andorrans had ceased complaining. Now when Jean-Pierre or Paul signalled that they needed to rest, they simply shrugged their shoulders, leaned against the nearest rock and began rolling more cigarettes.

They were high now, the autumn sun still warming but already descending towards the mountaintops. At another time Paul would have marvelled at the spectacular panoramic views: the sheer rock faces, the gigantic slabs of fallen limestone, the rugged crags and towering peaks. It was beautiful and breathtaking, and all so different to anywhere he had previously experienced. But he was too concerned about Jean-Pierre to enjoy the sights.

And now he was very tired, so tired that he was starting to lose track of time. He couldn't remember when he'd last slept; it was as though he'd been awake and walking for days.

To combat his overwhelming feeling of fatigue, Paul concentrated on keeping Jean-Pierre going, forcing everything else from his mind. But he realized now that he was fighting a losing battle.

Jean-Pierre looked terrible, exhausted and near to collapse. The most recent hike, past huge boulders and through a narrow pass, seemed to have sapped the last dregs of his strength, and when Paul offered him water and food, he could barely raise a hand to wave them away.

And since the pass, Paul had noticed that the trail had finally disappeared. There was nothing now to show the way, no track, no trodden footpath, no markers of any sort. All Paul and Jean-Pierre had to rely on now was the knowledge and experience of their guides.

The Andorrans were sitting huddled together, speaking quietly, a few metres from Paul and Jean-Pierre. Paul paid them little attention, relieved that at least they had stopped complaining.

They had been resting for about ten minutes when José

got to his feet and freed the shotgun slung across his back. He placed it on the ground close to his friends and ambled over to Paul and Jean-Pierre.

He nodded at Jean-Pierre. "How are you feeling?"

"Looking forward to seeing Spain," Jean-Pierre replied.

"I've been talking with my friends," the Andorran said, in better French than he had previously used. "We know you can't walk for much longer. But if you can keep going for another hour, no more than that, we'll reach an old hut; a mountain refuge. We'll stop there. You will rest. We'll cook some food and you can sleep. A good night's sleep and in the morning you'll be much stronger."

Jean-Pierre looked at Paul, a flicker of hope in his weary eyes. Paul too felt a sudden surge of optimism. The thought of hot food and somewhere to sleep, however uncomfortable, was almost too good to believe.

Jean-Pierre turned to the Andorran. "Just an hour more, you say?"

"An hour at the most, maybe less."

The high rocks on all sides masked the view of the way ahead. José pointed at one of them. "You can see the hut if we walk past that fallen rock," he said to Jean-Pierre. "Come, I'll show you."

"Let me go," Paul said, starting to get up.

"No," Jean-Pierre replied, rising unsteadily to his feet. "If I don't get up now I might never manage it again. You pack the food and water while I take a look."

Paul returned his smile. He was heavy with tiredness, but José's words had given him a fresh dose of confidence.

He watched Jean-Pierre follow José until they had passed the fallen rock. Then he gathered their things, not noticing the two remaining Andorrans studying him intently.

Jean-Pierre stepped through a gap between two rocks and the view opened up instantly. To his immediate right, fallen boulders more than two metres high clustered together at the bottom of a steeply rising rock face, but to his left a new panoramic expanse stretched towards a distant horizon.

The way ahead was narrow, just wide enough for one person to walk in relative safety. But to the left the path was little more than a long ledge, with a plummeting, almost sheer drop of hundreds of metres.

José glanced back, unconcerned. "Stay away from the edge. Don't look down; it can make you dizzy."

Jean-Pierre nodded, staying as close as he could to the rocks as he followed the Andorran. José strode on for a further twenty metres and halted. Here, to Jean-Pierre's relief, the track widened considerably into a small plateau.

José waited near the edge. "Come and look," he said, smiling. "You can see the hut from here."

Moving closer, Jean-Pierre was suddenly gripped by another coughing fit. He bent over, the coughs wracking his body.

The Andorran's smile disappeared as his right hand

began to reach into his sheepskin jerkin. But he instantly dropped his arm as Jean-Pierre stopped coughing and stood upright.

His smile returned. "Are you all right?"

"I'll be fine once we reach the refuge," Jean-Pierre said, moving to stand next to José, just a couple of paces from the edge and the terrifying drop.

"There," José said, pointing into the distance, "to your left. Look to the peak and then let your eyes come down. You'll see the hut."

Jean-Pierre stared, craning his neck forward, following the instructions, completely unaware than the Andorran's hand was reaching into his jerkin.

"Stop! Don't move!"

Jean-Pierre and José spun around.

Henri Mazet stepped out from a deep crevice in the rocks at the back of the plateau. He was staring down the barrels of a shotgun, which was pointed at the Andorran's chest.

"Henri!" Jean-Pierre gasped. "What ... what is...?"

"Get away from him, Jean-Pierre," Henri ordered. "Quickly!"

Jean-Pierre tried to step away, but not quickly enough. With lightning speed, the Andorran whipped a long-bladed knife from his jerkin, grabbed Jean-Pierre around the neck and held him fast with the blade against his throat.

"Drop the gun," he snarled at Henri. "Drop it, or I'll slit his throat here and now."

Henri hesitated, but his eyed blazed with determination. "And then what? No, you won't do it. You harm him and I swear I'll kill you. I swear it."

The Andorran looked startled at the ferocity of his words. But he didn't move.

"They're murderers, Jean-Pierre," Henri said. "Making their fortunes by killing and robbing escapees. But not this time." He glared at the Andorran. "Yvette tipped you off, didn't she?"

José said nothing. He grinned and pressed the knife against Jean-Pierre's flesh, hard enough to pierce the skin so that a thin trickle of blood ran down his neck.

"You'll get no more help from Yvette," Henri went on quickly. "Who was she? Your sister? Cousin? An old girlfriend?"

Still the Andorran said nothing.

"It doesn't matter," Henri continued. "She's dead now; you'll never hear from her again."

A look of hatred flashed across Jose's eyes, but still he stayed silent.

"Drop the knife," Henri ordered again. "Don't you see, it's all over."

They stood glaring at each other, both unwilling to back down. But then shouts pierced the thin mountain air and they all looked back towards the standing rocks where the path turned away from the plateau.

José laughed. "It's not over for me," he said to Henri,

"but it is for the boy. My friends are dealing with him now. Then they'll come to finish you two. Put down the gun, old man."

Jean-Pierre sagged, as though about to collapse, and José was forced to shift his feet slightly to keep his balance. It was the moment of opportunity Jean-Pierre was hoping for. In one sudden movement he raised both hands and clasped his captor's sheepskin jerkin.

"Help Paul, Henri!" he yelled. *"Help Paul!"*

Before José could react, Jean-Pierre pushed backward, summoning every bit of his remaining strength. The two men tottered on the ledge, the Andorran's eyes widening in terror as he tried frantically to stay upright.

They tipped back and then forward slightly, but Jean-Pierre somehow managed to push once more and Henri watched helplessly as the two men disappeared over the edge.

Henri heard the Andorran scream and a sickening thud as the falling bodies struck the first jagged outcrop of rocks. And then there was nothing. Only silence.

"Jean-Pierre," Henri breathed, still staring down the barrels of the shotgun.

More shouts cut through the air and Henri found himself hurtling towards the turn in the track.

FORTY

Henri sprinted, faster than he realized he could, perilously close to the crumbling edge. He reached the two standing rocks and stopped, panting, listening for voices or the sounds of a struggle. But he heard nothing, and once more Henri was struck by the agonizing thought that he was too late.

He raised the shotgun, bringing the wooden stock hard against his shoulder and edged slowly through the gap, fearing what he would see on the far side. But stepping into the open he gasped in shock at the sight that met his eyes.

Paul was alive and safe, and the two Andorrans had their arms raised in surrender. Didier had them covered by a shotgun held at his waist. And at Didier's side was Josette.

"Papa!" Josette yelled as she turned and saw Henri staring, relief and confusion in his eyes.

"But how … how did—?"

"I've been here before, Henri, remember?" Didier said, his eyes remaining on the two hostages. "I knew the way.

We were following, but we lost sight of you."

"I got ahead of them," Henri said, still looking bewildered, "where the path splits two ways. They stopped for Jean-Pierre."

"And Jean-Pierre," Paul asked urgently. "Where is he?"

Henri sighed and slowly shook his head.

"Oh," Josette breathed. "Oh, no."

Didier still had the Andorrans covered with the shotgun but his eyes were drawn to Henri. One of the two men glimpsed his chance and slowly began to bend his upstretched right arm at the elbow. His hand dipped behind his head and then slipped into the back of his jacket.

The hand emerged from a hidden pocket. Gripped tightly in the palm was a snub-nosed, semi-automatic Eibar pistol, old but deadly, particularly at short distances.

Spotting the movement, Paul looked back and saw the gun in the man's hand as he brought it over his head to aim and fire at Didier.

"Look out!" he shouted, flinging himself at the Andorran.

The pistol cracked and spat out a round. It ricocheted off the rock face, and Paul and the Andorran went crashing to the ground.

Paul's hand was locked onto the Andorran's arm. He clung on desperately, battling to get the fingers of his free hand onto the pistol as his opponent punched him, trying to force him to release his grip.

Didier could only look on, afraid to fire his gun for fear

of hitting Paul, unable to join the fight because of his own injured shoulder. Henri and Josette stood frozen in terror.

Paul was on his own.

He clung to the man's arm and they rolled over, their faces inches apart – so close that he could smell the garlic on his breath. But the Andorran was bigger and stronger, and gradually he turned the pistol to fire into Paul's body.

With no other option Paul drew back his head and viciously butted his opponent. There was an agonized scream as the man's nose shattered and blood spurted onto Paul's face. Paul felt as though his own skull had been cracked open.

The Andorran dropped the pistol and groped with both hands at his busted nose. Paul saw the weapon fall. Releasing his own grip, he rolled away and snatched the gun from the ground.

Head spinning, he got unsteadily to his feet, blood in his eyes, and at the same time, the enraged Andorran staggered up and ran towards him.

Didier was quickest to react. There was no way he could lift the shotgun to his damaged shoulder so he fired both barrels from the waist and was knocked back by the weapon's recoil.

The Andorran was hit in the chest. He spun away and slumped lifeless to the ground.

The thunderous roar of the shotgun echoed across the mountains and Didier's head dropped to his chest at the realization of what he had been forced to do. Josette stared, horrified, then she ran to her father, averting her eyes from the bloody scene.

Paul wiped the blood away from his eyes with the sleeve of his jacket. His sight restored, he saw the third Andorran crouch slightly, ready to leap at Didier.

"Stop!" Paul yelled.

The Andorran wheeled around and saw the pistol aimed at his heart. "No! No!" he shouted, raising his arms high and shaking his head to make it clear he had no intention of advancing.

Blood was streaming down Paul's face; his own as well as the dead man's. He blinked and dabbed at his face with his left hand.

Glimpsing a last chance, the Andorran decided to risk all.

He charged forward.

"Paul!" Josette screamed.

Through blurred vision Paul became aware of the shape hurtling towards him and heard a wild yell. He squeezed the trigger and felt the pistol's recoil.

When his vision cleared he saw the Andorran dead at his feet.

FORTY-ONE

"**P**aul!" Josette cried as she ran to him.

Paul said nothing. His eyes were on the lifeless Andorrans.

Josette moved closer to examine his wound. "It could have been worse," she said, examining the wound. "But you'll have a headache tomorrow." She handed him a clean handkerchief.

"I have one now," Paul answered, wiping away some of the blood.

Henri looked shattered. He took one hand from the shotgun, gripped Paul's arm and squeezed it tightly.

"Papa," Josette said gently, "will you please put down the gun. It doesn't suit you."

"It was my father's," Henri replied, releasing Paul's arm and breaking open the shotgun. "I must take it back."

He peered into the open barrels and then raised his eyebrows, lifting the weapon so that Paul and Josette could see clearly. "It's fortunate I didn't have to fire the thing," he said. "I forgot to load it."

Paul smiled. "Henri," he said, "how did you know what they planned to do?"

The mountain air was turning colder and Henri shivered. "I felt sure all along that something wasn't right. And then when Didier reminded me that Yvette was Andorran—"

"Yvette? What's she got to do with it?"

"Everything. She tipped off these men." He gestured towards Paul's suitcase. "There's a lot of money in there, much more than the remainder of their fee. They wanted it all. I suppose the deal was that they would share it with Yvette and the others once you and Jean-Pierre had been killed."

"The others?" Didier asked.

"I'll come to that." Henri turned back to Paul. "Yvette is dead. She paid the price for failing to kill Didier."

Paul stared. "It was Yvette?"

Henri nodded again and looked at his daughter. "You remember, Josette, that you told me how other people had been phoning the hospital to ask about Didier?"

Josette nodded.

"One of those callers would have been Yvette," Henri explained. "And when she learned that Didier would live she made the fatal mistake of telling the others that Didier saw her face when she pushed him into the machine."

"They killed her?" Josette said. "For that?"

"They knew that once she was questioned again she would reveal the whole story," Henri said. "Poor Yvette never could hold her tongue."

"And the others?" Paul asked again. "Who are they?"

Henri's eyes clouded, he seemed close to tears, stunned and saddened by the twists and turns and tragedies of the past few hours. "I can't be certain, but Gaston for one, I believe. It seems I didn't know my old friend as well as I thought."

"So I was right all along," Josette said. "He *is* a collaborator. And he *did* have Jean-Pierre arrested."

"Probably," Henri said, nodding. "When I told him we were going to free Jean-Pierre from Rivel he must have decided to dispose of both Paul and Jean-Pierre up here. Who knows, perhaps that end was already planned for Paul – but with two people escaping all the way to England, Gaston knew there would be even more cash in the suitcase. And they might have got away with it. Bodies can lay undiscovered in the mountains for years."

He sighed and shook his head. "Of course, I can't prove all this. We were told Gaston spent last night in Chalabre. Maybe he did, maybe it was a lie. Maybe he killed Yvette or maybe the killer was someone else."

"We have to find whoever did it," Paul said.

Henri raised his eyebrows again. "We?"

"Well, I can't leave now," Paul said, shrugging his shoulders, "it's impossible. None of us can follow the Eagle Trail onwards from here."

"Yes, he'll have to stay," Josette added quickly. "There's no other choice."

"And is that what you want?" Henri asked, looking at Paul closely.

Paul's reply was instant. "I want to stay. There's nothing for me to go back to in England. I can be of more use here; I want to help you find the traitors."

"And you, Didier," Henri said, "what do you think?"

Didier winced as a stab of pain reminded him of his injuries. "Well," he said, "he saved my life just now so I suppose we ought to let him stay."

"That's decided then," said Josette quickly. "And now, Papa, can we go home, please?"

"Yes," Henri said, "let's go home."

"But what about…?" Paul was looking at the two lifeless bodies on the ground. "We can't just leave them."

"You're right, Paul," Henri said. "But we can't take them with us, and we certainly can't bury them up here." He sighed heavily. "They'll have to join Jean-Pierre and their friend."

It took a few minutes to complete the gruesome task of disposing of the bodies and then, close to exhaustion, they turned to retrace their steps down the mountain track.

They walked in virtual silence; even Josette had no more to say as they concentrated on keeping their footing, picking their way along the narrow path.

Paul was at the rear of the straggling line, clutching the

battered suitcase he had carried with him since the first day of his flight from Antwerp. He walked in a daze, his thoughts jumbled and confused, when something, he didn't know what, made him look up into the sky.

He saw it immediately, the golden eagle soaring majestically, high above them. Floating, drifting, riding the thermals like a galleon in full sail.

"Jean-Pierre," Paul whispered, his mind suddenly clear, "I'm sorry we'll never get to see the Tower of London together."

And then, as he watched, the golden eagle turned towards the setting sun. Flying powerfully, flying fast, flying upward.

Upward.

ACKNOWLEDGEMENTS

My thanks to all those who helped, in many ways, during the research and writing of *The Eagle Trail*. Special thanks to Philippe Vidal, Louis Vives, Richard and Dorothy Vaughton, Jan and Nigel Watson, Peter Phelps, and to the late Paul René Simon.

I would also like to thank my editor, Mara Bergman, and everyone at Walker Books, and my agents, Vivien Green and Janet Fillingham. Finally, and most of all, I want to thank my wife, Carolyn. For everything.

Robert Rigby